PUFFIN BOOKS

The Hero P-

Praise for

'If you love Micha   , you'll
enjoy this' *Sunday Express*

'A moving tale told with warmth, kindliness and
lashings of good sense that lovers of Dick King-Smith
will especially appreciate' *The Times*

'Every now and then a writer comes along with a unique
way of storytelling. Meet Megan Rix . . . her novels are
deeply moving and will strike a chord with animal lovers'
LoveReading

'A perfect story for animal lovers and lovers of adventure
stories' Travelling Book Company

Praise from Megan's young readers

'I never liked reading until one day I was in
Waterstones and I picked up some books. One was . . .
called *The Bomber Dog*. I loved it so much I couldn't
put it down' Luke, 8

'I found this book amazing' Nayah, 11

'EPIC BOOK!!!' Jessica, 13

'One of my favourite books' Chloe, Year 8

MEGAN RIX is the recent winner of the Stockton and Shrewsbury Children's Book Awards, and has been shortlisted for numerous other children's book awards. She lives with her husband by a river in England. When she's not writing she can be found walking her two golden retrievers, Traffy and Bella, who are often in the river.

Books by Megan Rix

THE BOMBER DOG

THE GREAT ESCAPE

THE HERO PUP

A SOLDIER'S FRIEND

THE VICTORY DOGS

www.meganrix.com

The Hero Pup

megan rix

PUFFIN

PUFFIN BOOKS

Published by the Penguin Group
Penguin Books Ltd, 80 Strand, London WC2R ORL, England
Penguin Group (USA) Inc., 375 Hudson Street, New York, New York 10014, USA
Penguin Group (Canada), 90 Eglinton Avenue East, Suite 700, Toronto, Ontario,
Canada M4P 2Y3 (a division of Pearson Penguin Canada Inc.)
Penguin Ireland, 25 St Stephen's Green, Dublin 2, Ireland (a division of Penguin Books Ltd)
Penguin Group (Australia), 707 Collins Street, Melbourne, Victoria 3008, Australia
(a division of Pearson Australia Group Pty Ltd)
Penguin Books India Pvt Ltd, 11 Community Centre, Panchsheel Park, New Delhi – 110 017, India
Penguin Group (NZ), 67 Apollo Drive, Rosedale, Auckland 0632, New Zealand
(a division of Pearson New Zealand Ltd)
Penguin Books (South Africa) (Pty) Ltd, Block D, Rosebank Office Park,
181 Jan Smuts Avenue, Parktown North, Gauteng 2193, South Africa

Penguin Books Ltd, Registered Offices: 80 Strand, London WC2R ORL, England

puffinbooks.com

First published 2014
001

Text Copyright © Megan Rix, 2014
Illustrations copyright © Puffin Books, 2014
Illustrations by Sara Chadwick-Holmes
All rights reserved

The moral right of the author has been asserted

Set in 13/20 pt Baskerville MT Std
Typeset by Jouve (UK), Milton Keynes
Printed in Great Britain by Clays Ltd, St Ives plc

British Library Cataloguing in Publication Data
A CIP catalogue record for this book is available from the British Library

ISBN: 978-0-141-35192-6

www.greenpenguin.co.uk

A tribute to all Helpful Dogs and their human friends . . .

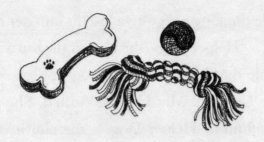

Chapter 1

Marnie, a five-year-old yellow Labrador, stood at the front door and gave a single bark. When no one came, she sat down and waited for a few seconds, then awkwardly stood up again and waddled down the hallway. She went into the kitchen, past the small table, over to the glass back door that led out to the garden, whined and looked behind her.

Grey-haired Mrs Hodges was seated at the kitchen table. She heard Marnie's whine, but didn't look up from reading the local newspaper while dunking a digestive biscuit into her mug of tea. 'Helper Dogs' she read at the top of the article that had a large photograph of some dogs below it. Mrs Hodges smiled. She was very fond of Helper Dogs – the charity that trained dogs to help people with special needs. Her friend Lenny ran the local centre not far away. They were looking for more volunteer puppy raisers and suitable puppies to be donated to the charity.

Marnie whined again and then gave a short, sharp bark. Mrs Hodges finally looked up and found herself being stared at by her dog's soft brown eyes.

Mrs Hodges knew full well what that stare meant.

'You wouldn't think a dog in your condition would still want to be heading out for walks. Those puppies are going to come along very soon,' she said as she put the newspaper down and stood up.

Marnie stepped from one front paw to the other to ease the weight in her belly, her claws making tapping sounds on the wooden floor.

'Just a small one then.'

Marnie's thick tail wagged as she followed Mrs Hodges to the front door and waited for her to take down the lead from the hook she kept it on. Being pregnant didn't stop Marnie from wanting to go for a walk, but it did mean the walks had to be much shorter – and no free runs or trips in the car.

'Come on then,' Mrs Hodges said as she opened the front door.

Outside, the sun was shining. It was a bright summer's day with a clear blue sky. Marnie hurried out as fast as she could waddle. 'Slowly now,' Mrs Hodges warned her.

The old lady kept a careful eye on Marnie during their gentle walk round the block. She'd been through it all before and knew that Marnie's instinct was to find a place to give birth outdoors. Mrs Hodges' instinct, however, was to help choose Marnie's birthing spot for her – indoors, where she could keep a close eye on things.

But Marnie was surprisingly quick for a heavily pregnant dog.

'Come out of there!' Mrs Hodges cried as Marnie dived under a promising-looking hedge. She'd only just managed to coax the Labrador back out when a long black car drove slowly past them. They both turned to watch the hearse pass. In the back, resting on the coffin, was a wreath of white and purple flowers that spelt the word DAD.

'Oh dear,' muttered Mrs Hodges, bowing her head and giving Marnie a pat.

Behind the hearse was a black limousine. As it passed them by, Mrs Hodges caught a glimpse of a sandy-haired boy in the back seat, staring determinedly straight ahead. Marnie barked and for a brief second the boy looked over at them.

'Poor love,' Mrs Hodges said as she and Marnie continued on their walk.

After the funeral was over everyone – or it seemed like everyone – came back to eleven-year-old Joe Scott's house. Not that Joe wanted them there, but that's what his mum said people did.

He went into his room to get away from them, but people kept knocking on his door and poking their heads round it to ask if he was OK.

Of course I'm not, he wanted to scream at them. *Why would I be OK?* He'd never be OK.

There was a large cupboard with a lattice door on one side of his bedroom. Joe picked up his phone, opened the door, stepped inside the cupboard, closed the door behind him and sat down on the floor among his shoes.

Then someone else knocked on his bedroom door and walked in. 'Joe?'

Joe didn't reply and soon he heard the footsteps retreating.

Without thinking, Joe studied his phone. He had lots of photos of Dad on it and he scrolled slowly through them. He didn't like looking at the ones of Dad in his army uniform the last time they'd said goodbye. He scrolled back to the ones of them together from before: Christmas last year, way before Dad told him that he'd be going away; him and his dad both wearing Cat in the Hat hats.

Christmas. Joe's stomach flipped over. He didn't want to have a Christmas without Dad.

Joe's favourite photo was of him and his dad laughing together on holiday at the beach in July, just over a year ago.

He carried on looking at the photos until finally the house became quiet.

Then suddenly the cupboard door opened and Joe jerked his head up. His mum stood there. She'd kicked off the high-heeled black shoes she'd worn for the funeral.

'It's not fair,' Joe said.

'I know it isn't.'

'Why did it have to be him?'

His mum had no answer. There *was* no answer. She held her hand out to pull Joe up, but he didn't take it immediately.

'I don't want to go back.'

'Back where?'

'To school after the holidays.' His voice caught in his throat. 'The other kids will ask me about Dad.'

He didn't want to talk about the funeral with anyone, and especially not with nosy-parker people. He loved his dad too much for that, and the ache he felt every time he thought about how much he missed him had left a hole so big it felt like he could crawl inside it and stay there forever.

'Come on, let's have some food,' his mum said, offering her hand again.

'I'm not hungry,' he told her as she pulled him up.

'Then help me clear it all away.'

Mrs Hodges filled Marnie's bowl with the special food for dogs who are expecting puppies, but Marnie wouldn't touch it. She hadn't been interested in food all day, which wasn't at all like the usual Marnie.

'Well, I suppose that's to be expected. Shouldn't think it will be long now,' Mrs Hodges told the Labrador as she softly stroked Marnie's bulging belly. The old lady had taken to feeding the dog near the nesting box where she tried to get Marnie to sleep too. Much better for the puppies to be born there than under some bush that took Marnie's fancy.

Marnie liked the stroking and she fell asleep in the special box Mrs Hodges had made for her, snoring loudly. The snoring, loud as it was, was oddly soothing. Mrs Hodges hadn't slept properly over the last few nights. She'd had one ear open for any sound that might mean Marnie was about to give birth. Now she carried on stroking the snoring dog until they'd both nodded off.

Marnie hadn't been asleep for more than an hour when her eyes opened and she gave a yelp.

Mrs Hodges woke up too and rubbed her eyes. 'Goodness! Is it time?' she asked. Then she looked properly at Marnie and smiled as the first of the puppies was born. Five more followed over the next few hours.

'What a clever girl you are, Marnie. Six puppies!' Mrs Hodges said as she checked each of the newborns.

There were four boys and two girls, and all of the pups were completely yellow except for one of the boys who had a patch of black on his right ear.

'There'll be no mistaking you, will there, little Patch,' Mrs Hodges said as she cleaned the black-eared puppy with a soft towel. Patch made a high mewling sound, almost as if he'd heard her. But he hadn't. Newborn puppies are all blind and deaf, but have a strong sense of smell. Patch's tiny pink nose pressed against Mrs Hodges's thumb and she put him with his mum so he could feed.

Mrs Hodges had given all the other puppies a dot on the top of the head, using different coloured marker pens to identify them. The puppy born straight after Patch was the last of the litter and smaller than the others.

'You'll soon catch up with the rest of them, Little Blue,' Mrs Hodges told her as she marked the top of the puppy's head with a blue dot.

Once she was sure that there were no more puppies to come, Mrs Hodges picked up the little dog with the black ear and smiled as he made the mewling sound again and tried to suck her finger. She'd heard of these sorts of markings occurring in pure-bred Labradors before – mosaic puppies they were called – but she'd never seen it for herself.

'Well, you'll never win a dog show with that ear, Patch,' she told the puppy. 'I'm not even sure I'll be able to sell you. But I know somewhere that'll take you with open arms, somewhere that you'll become the most precious puppy in the world. I'll give my friend Lenny a call just as soon as I get a chance and see what he has to say.'

She put Patch back in the nesting box and he snuggled up to his mum with his brothers and sisters.

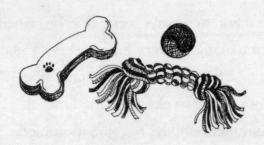

Chapter 2

Joe was sitting in the sunshine on a bit of broken brick wall at the end of the garden. Inside the house, up in her office with the window open, he could hear his mum talking on the phone to someone, but not the actual words she was saying.

'Why aren't you at school?' a gruff voice suddenly asked, making Joe jump.

It was their next-door neighbour, grumpy Mr Humphreys, pretending to be trimming the hedge by the wall but really spying on them. He was always at home because he was retired and he always seemed to be criticizing Joe or making not very funny jokes. 'You don't look sick. Should I call the truant officer?'

It was three weeks since the funeral.

'Summer holidays . . .' Joe mumbled.

'What's that you're saying? Speak up, young man!' barked Mr Humphreys.

'It's the summer –' Joe started to say again, when his mum called out from the back door.

'Joe! Joe, come quickly!'

Mr Humphreys watched as Joe sighed and walked slowly back inside with his head down. 'Sad-looking lad,' he muttered, then went back to his hedge-chopping.

'What is it?' Joe asked his mum as he came in from the garden.

'Remember how you always wanted a dog?' she said breathlessly.

'Yes. But . . .' Last Christmas Dad had said this might be the year they got one. Only then he'd got the news about going away on tour with his regiment and getting a dog had been forgotten. His mum couldn't be getting them a dog, could she? Joe didn't know what to think about that. Having a dog had always been something he and Dad had talked about.

'But I thought you and Dad decided it would be too much work with Dad away, and now . . .' Joe trailed off.

'Well there might be a way,' she said.

'What – how?'

'Come on, we're going out,' Mum announced suddenly.

'Mum, I'm not sure . . .' Joe had hardly been out at all in the few weeks since the funeral. He didn't want to see anyone and he certainly didn't want to talk to anyone.

'Hurry up. We don't want to be late.'

'Late for what?' Joe asked, following her as she almost ran out of the front door.

'Our meeting at Helper Dogs.'

'What meeting? What's Helper Dogs?'

'The meeting I've just arranged. Hurry, because I can't leave the office for too long.'

Joe's mum worked for a telecommunications company from home. She used the back bedroom as her office, which had all been set up by the company. The firm had given her a computer to work on and also a separate phone for her work calls. She answered customers' queries and set up new accounts. Mostly she worked office hours, but she could log out for an hour or so, provided she let her manager know.

'The best bit about working from home is I can work in my pyjamas if I feel like it,' she told people. But Joe had never seen her wearing her pyjamas all day – not once.

'What's Helper Dogs?' Joe asked again as they got in the car.

'It's only five minutes away. You'll soon see,' she said mysteriously.

After what felt like much longer to Joe, his mum eventually slowed the car down and turned into a long driveway with what looked like a small aircraft hangar at the end of it. She pulled into the car park and was out of the car in no time. Joe followed more slowly. He was still not quite sure exactly what was going on.

'Hello!' Joe's mum called, breezing into the hangar as if she went there every day.

A golden retriever with a wagging tail came over to greet them. The dog was followed by a bald-headed man in jeans and a polo shirt that said HELPER DOGS on it.

'Mary, hello, great to see you – and you must be Joe, right?' he said.

Joe looked at his feet. Why had Mum brought him here? He didn't want to talk to anyone, especially not new people.

'Yes,' said Mum for him. 'This is Joe.'

'I'm Lenny; pleased to meet you,' said the man. Joe continued to stare at his feet, but jumped suddenly as he felt something cold and a little bit wet touch his hand. He looked down to find the golden retriever giving his hand a lick.

Lenny laughed. 'That's Ollie. Don't mind him, he's just saying hello. Did the same thing to your dad when he came to see me.'

Joe finally looked up at the man. His dad had come here.

'Ollie's one of the first Helper Dogs I trained and I can't tell you how pleased I was to have him back once he retired,' Lenny explained.

'What's a Helper Dog?' Joe asked.

'Exactly what it sounds like – a dog that helps,' Lenny told him. 'Do you want to see some of the helpful things Ollie can do?'

Joe looked at Mum, who nodded.

'OK,' said Joe.

'Lights, Ollie,' Lenny said, pointing to a long cord hanging from the ceiling by the wall.

Ollie trotted over and pulled the cord and the lights came on.

'That's amazing,' said Joe's mum.

'He can also press an ordinary light switch on the wall with his paw to turn the lights on. But I don't get him to do that so often now he's older because it's harder on his hips.'

Ollie went over and nudged Lenny's pocket and Lenny rolled his eyes, pulled out a treat and gave it to him.

'Now I'm using him as a demonstration dog he wants a treat for every little thing he does,' Lenny laughed. 'Sometimes I give him a treat, but sometimes I just give him a bit of his food.'

Ollie swallowed down the treat and looked up hopefully for more.

'Could you call this number on your phone?' Lenny said, and he gave Joe's mum a piece of paper. She rang the number and a phone started ringing. Lenny looked round. 'Where is it?' he asked Ollie, holding his hands up to show he didn't know where the phone could be. 'Find it.'

Ollie trotted over to the table and then disappeared underneath it, grabbed the phone in his mouth and came trotting back to Lenny with it, his tail wagging.

'Thank you,' Lenny said to Ollie when the dog reached him. He took the phone from him. 'Hello.'

'Hello,' Joe's mum replied into her phone.

Joe found himself smiling.

Ollie looked up at Lenny for his treat and Lenny obliged.

Then Lenny said, 'Grab a chair,' to Joe and his mum, and he sat down himself. 'Now, imagine I'm in a wheelchair or don't have much mobility – that's to say, I can't move very easily and reaching my shoes to take them off can be really awkward, and for some people just about impossible. Give it a try – without moving your legs.'

Joe bent over and tried to reach his shoes without moving his legs at all, remembering he was pretending to be in a wheelchair and didn't want to fall out. It wasn't easy.

'Shoes, Ollie,' Lenny said, pointing at his feet. Lenny was wearing trainers with Velcro straps and Ollie pulled back the Velcro. 'He can also pull the laces undone if they're tied in a single bow.'

Next, with a little help from Lenny pushing at the shoe with his other foot, Ollie managed to pull both of Lenny's shoes completely off.

'Well done,' Lenny said. 'Socks next.'

Ollie carefully took hold of the very edge of the toe of Lenny's sock and pulled.

'Helps if you wear loose socks,' Lenny added, laughing as Ollie braced his legs and pulled. The first sock was off in no time. Ollie turned his attention to the second sock and soon that one was off too.

Ollie wagged his tail.

'It's all a big game to the dogs,' Lenny said, giving Ollie a bit of his dog-food kibble as a

treat. 'And that's just the way we want it to be.'
He pulled his socks and shoes back on and
when Ollie went to take them off all over again,
Lenny said, 'No, no, once is quite enough,
thank you! Get my hat.' Lenny tapped his head
and Ollie ran to the table, picked up a woolly
hat and brought it back to Lenny, dropping it
in his lap. 'Thank you,' Lenny said as he put
it on.

'I never knew a dog could do all those things!'
Joe said.

'That's not even the half of what he can do,'
Lenny told him. 'Not even a quarter in fact.'

'Joe, we're here because I thought maybe we
could become volunteers for Helper Dogs,'
Joe's mum said.

'I gather you've always wanted a dog,' Lenny
said, smiling at him.

'Well, it was really Dad and me who always
wanted a dog, so I'm not sure . . .' said Joe, his
voice trailing off.

'Joe, it's actually something Dad and I talked about with Lenny a long time ago,' Joe's mum explained gently.

'Your dad and mum came here back in May to see whether it might be possible. We're always looking for volunteers to be puppy raisers, you see. We pay all the bills.'

'So . . . the puppy would live with us?' Joe asked his mum, hardly able to believe it. Had his dad wanted a dog from Lenny?

'Yes – it'd live with you until it went on for further training or to live with the person it's being partnered with.'

'How long would it live with us?' Joe's mum asked.

'Well, it depends on the puppy and how quickly it learns, and who it is going to go to. It can be anything from a few months to a year. Volunteers need to be at home during the day as the puppy shouldn't be left alone for long periods of time.'

'That'd be cruel,' Joe said, and Lenny nodded.

'Most of the dogs trained by Helper Dogs go to live with disabled adults, many of whom have been injured in the armed services. That's how your dad first heard about us, through his work,' explained Lenny. 'In fact, only this morning I had a phone call from the military hospital about a disabled soldier called Sam Hilling who'd like a Helper Dog.'

'What happened to him?' Joe wanted to know despite his mum giving him a meaningful look.

Lenny sighed. 'He went back to rescue some of his men from a house that had been bombed – and a wall collapsed on him.'

'Oh no,' Joe's mum said, bringing her hand to her mouth.

'He survived against all the odds, but will never walk again. A Helper Dog could really make all the difference to his recovery and his ability to lead a normal life.'

'What do you think then?' asked Joe's mum. Joe thought about it for a moment. He took a deep breath.

'I'd like to help,' he said.

Ollie came over to him and nuzzled his hand.

'Good,' Lenny said. 'It'll be an awful lot of work, you know; you won't see much of the summer holidays because you'll need to come along to lots of training classes before you get the puppy.'

'We've never had a dog before, and I don't have any experience,' Joe's mum said.

'That's what the training classes are for,' Lenny explained. 'Plus we'll need to make sure your house and garden are puppy friendly. Are you sure you're both really interested? It'll take a lot of dedication and there's not much sleep for the first few weeks once you do get the puppy.'

Joe looked at his mum and their eyes met. Was this really something Dad had planned for them?

'We're interested,' Joe's mum said, smiling, and Joe nodded.

'Would you like to meet the puppy I'm hoping we'll be able to use for Sam once it's old enough?' Lenny asked them. 'The breeder lives not far from here.'

Joe nodded again. 'Yes, I would.'

'I'm afraid I need to get back to work,' Joe's mum said. 'Sorry, but I said I'd be back within the hour.'

'I can drop Joe off afterwards,' Lenny told her.

'Great – see you later, Joe.' She gave his arm a quick squeeze and then waved goodbye as she left.

'Keys, Ollie,' Lenny said, and Ollie trotted over to the table, picked up Lenny's keys and brought them back to him.

Joe couldn't wait to meet the puppy, but he also felt nervous. Everything seemed to be happening so fast. What if the puppy didn't like him? It was supposed to be him and Dad doing this together. Joe didn't know anything about dogs, let alone puppies. He'd never even taken a dog for a walk on his own before. What if it all went horribly wrong?

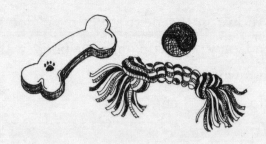

Chapter 3

Lenny's van had HELPER DOGS written on the side of it. Ollie jumped in the back as Joe pulled open the passenger door. The van smelt of wet dogs, and there were old dog toys and bits of half-eaten dog chews in it as well as lots of drink cans and sweet wrappers.

'Sorry about the mess,' Lenny apologized, but Joe didn't mind a bit.

Lenny drove back the same way that Joe and his mum had driven to Helper Dogs.

'We live in the next street over,' Joe said when Lenny pulled up outside a house with an overgrown garden.

'No, really?' Lenny said.

'Yep.'

Ollie wanted to get out of the car and visit too, but Lenny wouldn't let him.

'Sorry, old boy, but you'll only stress the mother dog if you come in,' he said, finding a bit of chew for Ollie to gnaw on while they were away. Ollie made a doggie grumble sound, but he didn't try to get out of the van again.

Joe followed Lenny through the gate and up the path. Lenny rang the doorbell and Mrs Hodges opened it, closely followed by Marnie, who always liked to know who was coming in and out.

'Good to see you, Lenny,' Mrs Hodges said.

'You too. This is Joe, our newest volunteer, hopefully.'

'Come in, come in; get out of the way, Marnie,' said Mrs Hodges as she pushed the dog back. But Marnie still managed to push her head under Joe's hand so he could stroke her as her tail wagged in welcome.

Mrs Hodges led Joe and Lenny down the passage and into the kitchen, where the puppies were in their playpen. Joe stood in the doorway and gasped at the sight of them. He didn't think he'd ever seen anything so beautiful. The six yellow puppies were lying huddled together – some of them half on top of each other, others nose to nose. Every now and again one of them would make a little sleepy sound, while another made a sucking noise in his sleep.

'You can come closer than that,' Mrs Hodges said, and Joe walked over to the playpen and looked down. 'They're still a bit tired,' she told him, 'and full up from being fed. But they'll be bouncing around again in no time. You wouldn't believe how much energy a three-week-old puppy has once it gets going!'

No sooner had she spoken than one of the puppies yawned, stood up sleepily, walked a few paces, and then flopped back down again.

'They're born with their eyes and ears closed,' Mrs Hodges told Joe. 'And for the first few weeks they mostly eat and sleep and poop.'

Joe couldn't take his eyes off them. He'd wanted a puppy for so long and now he was finally going to have one.

Mrs Hodges pointed to a puppy with a black ear, and a much smaller puppy, smaller than any of the others, lying next to it.

'That's Patch and Little Blue – they mostly sleep curled up together. Best of friends, those two.'

'Can they walk when they're born, like horses and deer, or are they like human babies?' Joe asked as he looked down at the sleeping pups.

'When they're about two weeks old, same time as their eyes and ears open, they learn to paddle-crawl and then to crawl properly. That's when they get a lot noisier and *nosier* too. They'd be into everything if you let them,' Mrs Hodges told him as she pressed her lips together.

The puppies were all waking up now and the black-eared one headed over to Joe.

'You can hold him if you like,' Mrs Hodges said as she reached into the pen and picked Patch up.

'I'm not sure . . . What if I drop him?' Joe asked anxiously.

'Sit on the floor and I'll pass him to you,' Mrs Hodges said.

'I don't know how . . .' Joe hesitated before slowly sitting down cross-legged on the kitchen tiles.

'You'll be just fine; they're quite tough little things, although they can be wriggly. Ready?' And she placed the puppy in his lap.

Joe had never felt fur so soft before. He could feel Patch's little heart beating very fast as he held him.

Then Patch stood on his back legs and stretched up to look straight into Joe's eyes. Joe smiled back into his.

'Hello, Patch,' he said quietly.

The other puppies followed Patch over to the side of the pen, all wanting to see who the strangers were.

'I've set up a pen for the puppies in the garden as it's such a nice day,' Mrs Hodges said. 'It'll be their first time outside. Pretty exciting for a puppy. You bring Patch, Joe, and I should be able to manage three, and Lenny, can you bring the last two? Puppies can be very wriggly, Joe.'

As soon as they went through the back door, Patch's little nose started sniffing the air and he sneezed with excitement. Joe carefully put him down in the playpen and he strutted about with his nose up, still sniffing the unfamiliar surroundings. Mrs Hodges put the first and second of her three puppies into the pen to join him. But when she went to put Little Blue down, the puppy was so excited that she wriggled away and the next moment was running down the garden rather than scampering safely in the pen with the others.

'Quickly, grab her!' Mrs Hodges exclaimed.

But it was too late. Blue had run straight into the compost heap, rolled in it, and was now covered in potato peelings and slimy green stuff.

'Phew!' Joe said as he picked the puppy up. Little Blue smelt terrible.

'It would be you, wouldn't it!' Mrs Hodges said to Little Blue. 'She may be the smallest, but she's got the strongest will. So determined! Keep hold of her, Joe. The first of the prospective owners are coming to see the puppies this afternoon so she'll need a bath.

I'll just fill the washing-up bowl and bring it out here. Luckily she's small enough to fit in it.'

Little Blue tried to wriggle away from Joe to join Patch in the pen, but Joe held on to her firmly and didn't let go.

A minute later Mrs Hodges came out with the washing-up bowl full of warm water, some puppy shampoo and a soft towel.

Little Blue loved splashing about in the warm water and Joe thought she wasn't even the least bit sorry for getting all smelly if it meant she got to splash about. Once all the slime was washed off, Mrs Hodges dried her with the soft towel.

'Little Minx should be your name,' she told the puppy, who wagged her tail with delight.

Joe shook his head and Lenny grinned. They both knew that Mrs Hodges didn't mean a word of it. She had a soft spot for the naughty little puppy.

Patch and Little Blue hurried towards each other as soon as Mrs Hodges had dried the smallest pup and put her safely in the playpen. They pressed their heads together, flopped on to the ground together and rolled about before jumping up again.

'Patch and Blue have been best friends right from the start,' Mrs Hodges told Joe as he watched the two puppies playing together. 'First one of them would lead and then the other would be in front. They were born straight after each other and I like to think of them as friends from birth – maybe even before birth,' she added.

Then Mrs Hodges gave Joe each of the other four puppies to hold in turn.

'The more they get used to it, the less frightened they'll be,' she said.

'They don't seem frightened,' Joe said as he held each warm puppy on his lap.

'That's because they know they've got nothing to be frightened of with you,' Mrs Hodges told him.

Joe was sure that couldn't be true. Little puppies couldn't really know, could they? But he liked what she said.

'We'd better be heading off,' Lenny said half an hour later. 'Puppies'll need feeding and there're more dog classes to teach and paperwork to do back at Helper Dogs.'

'Where do you live, Joe?' Mrs Hodges asked him. 'You look familiar.'

'Just round the corner,' Joe told her.

'Well then, you must come back to see the puppies any time you like.'

'Can I?' Joe said. 'Can I really? Could I bring my mum? She had to work today.' He looked at Patch and knew his mum would fall in love with him too as soon as she met him.

'Yes, of course you can bring her. The more the puppies get used to being handled and played with before they leave me, the better. Bring your dad along too, if you want.'

Joe's stomach turned over. He could feel his face going hot and red and he looked down at his feet. Suddenly Mrs Hodges remembered the funeral car she'd seen that day, right before the puppies were born. That's where she'd seen him before. Poor boy. Had the funeral car she'd seen him in been for his dad?

'Um, my dad's . . .' Joe started to say.

'I think it's time we were getting home,' Lenny said quickly. 'I'll be back with Joe for Patch's test in a fortnight. In the meantime,' he said to Joe, 'you've got a lot of learning to do to make sure you're ready for him! It's going to be hard work, but I'm sure you can do it. You'll need to come back to the Helper Dogs training centre over the next two weeks to learn more about looking after Patch.'

Joe looked up at Lenny. 'I'll come every day, if you like, and after Patch's test. At least until school starts . . .' he added quietly. School. Joe didn't want to think about it. A month to go.

Ollie was looking out of the driver's window when they got back to the van. 'No need to give me a lift,' Joe said. 'I only live round the corner, remember.'

'OK,' Lenny said. 'See you in the morning.'

Joe waved to Mrs Hodges and Marnie, who were standing at the door.

'See you soon,' he said.

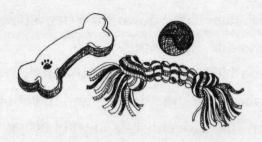

Chapter 4

Joe couldn't wait to tell his mum all about meeting Patch and the other puppies, and he ran all the way home.

Mr Humphreys was trimming his front garden hedge as Joe sprinted past.

'Slow down – you'll do yourself a mischief running like that, lad,' he said.

But Joe didn't stop. He ran up the path and unlocked the front door. Mr Humphreys shook his head and went back to his trimming.

'Mum, I'm back!' Joe yelled.

His mum came down from her office. 'So how was it?' she asked.

'You have to see them! Mrs Hodges and Marnie – that's the breeder and the puppies' mum – they live only one street over,' Joe said breathlessly. 'We can see them whenever we like. I want to see them every day!'

'That might be a bit much,' his mum warned. 'Mrs Hodges will be very busy and she's already had you and Lenny visiting her today.'

'I won't get in the way,' Joe insisted. 'I can help. You need lots of hands to look after them.'

He told his mum about Little Blue's race for the compost heap and then he told her about Patch.

'You won't be able to help but love him. He's just about the best puppy in the whole world!'

Joe headed into the kitchen to get a drink and Joe's mum followed him, smiling at his excitement. This was the first time he'd managed to raise a smile since his father had died.

The following day, after Mum had finished her work hours for the day, they both went back to Mrs Hodges' house. Joe rang the doorbell and Mrs Hodges opened it, Marnie peeping round from behind her legs to see who was there.

'We don't want to be a nuisance,' Joe's mum said, 'but Joe told me about Patch and I'd really like to see the puppies, if it's not too inconvenient. We don't have your phone number so we couldn't –' Mrs Hodges ushered them in before Joe's mum had even finished speaking, and Marnie nudged Joe's hand and got the strokes she'd been waiting for.

'It's no bother at all,' Mrs Hodges said. 'The puppies are just about to have their dinner. They're learning to eat soaked dry food rather than just their mother's milk and it can get very messy. They seem to think the food's for bathing in as well as for eating. Two extra pairs of hands will come in very useful indeed.'

Patch was fast asleep, curled up with his head resting on one of the star-shaped soft-rag toys Mrs Hodges had put in the puppy pen for them to play with when the doorbell had rung. He stretched his puppy legs and gave a sleepy yawn, but didn't open his eyes until he smelt a familiar smell. It was a smell that made him happy. A smell that made his little heart race. Then he heard Joe's voice as he came into the kitchen and Patch scrambled up and hurried over to the side of the puppy pen, his tail wagging.

'Oh,' Joe's mum exclaimed when she saw him. 'Oh, he's beautiful. Hello, Patch,' she said as she crouched down.

Joe lifted Patch out of his pen and hugged him as the excited puppy licked his face and made him laugh.

'Dad would love him,' Joe said as he gave Patch to his mum to hold for the first time.

Joe's mum's voice cracked. 'Yes, he would,' she said as she buried her face in Patch's soft fur.

'Would you like to help me get their food ready for them, Joe?' Mrs Hodges asked.

Joe nodded. Under Mrs Hodges's instruction he tipped the dry puppy food into a blender, added some puppy milk replacer and water, then whizzed it all up before pouring it into the large round metal feeder tray that all the puppies ate from.

'How often do you feed them?' Joe's mum asked as she stroked Patch on her lap.

'Four times a day usually,' Mrs Hodges told her. 'I'll gradually increase the amount of dry puppy food and decrease the milk and blend it less until they're just eating the puppy food by the time they leave me to go to their new homes.'

Joe and his mum exchanged a look. They both wanted Patch's new home to be their home.

Mum put Patch back with his brothers and sisters as Joe carefully placed the full food tray in the middle of the pen. All the puppies waddled or ran over to it. They made noisy slurping sounds as they gulped the food down.

'That's good,' Mrs Hodges remarked from the sink where she was dampening some flannels. 'They're getting the idea that the tray is for eating from rather than paddling in.'

Once the six puppies had had enough food, Marnie finished off what was left and licked the tray clean.

Joe picked up Patch again and held him in his arms, wiping his furry face with one of the damp flannels as the puppy's little tail wagged. Joe's mum wiped the face and paws of a friendly, cuddly, sleepy larger pup with a pink dot on his head, and Mrs Hodges cleaned Little Blue.

'You, young lady, got more food in your fur than in your stomach,' she told her.

Joe grinned. Mrs Hodges, for all her complaining about Little Blue, definitely had a soft spot for her.

'Put Patch on the newspaper now,' Mrs Hodges warned Joe. 'Puppies need to *go* almost as soon as they've eaten. Food goes right through them at this age.'

They'd only just finished cleaning the puppies when the doorbell rang again and Mrs Hodges, followed by Marnie, went to see who it was while Joe and his mum kept an eye on Marnie's brood.

'When I told them we were getting a puppy they just couldn't wait . . .' The speaker was a woman accompanied by two little girls of about four and five years old. They all followed Mrs Hodges into the kitchen.

'I don't blame them; getting a puppy is very exciting,' Mrs Hodges replied. 'They're over here.'

The little girls immediately spotted Patch with his distinctive black ear.

'Oh, look at him!'

'He's so sweet.'

'Can we get this one, Mum, please . . . ?'

Joe's heart sank. What if Mrs Hodges sold Patch to a family instead of letting Helper Dogs have him?

Mrs Hodges turned from the counter where she'd been pouring glasses of squash for the girls.

'Which one is that?' she asked them.

'The one with the black ear.'

Mrs Hodges looked over at Joe. 'Sorry,' she said. 'That one's already been picked. But you can hold him if you like.'

The girls both wanted to hold Patch and took it in turns to pet him. The puppy loved to be cuddled, but after a little while he wanted to go back with his brothers and sisters and he started to squirm and make mewling sounds.

They put wriggling Patch back in the pen and he ran over to Little Blue, and they were soon playing chase and gently biting each other's ears.

'Why's one of his ears black?' the older girl asked.

'He was just born like that. It's called a genetic mismark and happens sometimes in pure-breds. It means that Patch, as I call him, won't win any dog shows, but I've got other, bigger, plans for him.'

'What plans?' the girls wanted to know.

'Well Patch is very smart and he has a sweet nature too, as you've found out.'

The girls nodded.

'So I'm hoping he'll become a Helper Dog one day, as long as he passes the test. And Joe and his mum are going to help train him.'

'What's a Helper Dog?' the girls asked.

'A dog that does helpful things for disabled people,' Joe's mum explained.

'For now he'll just be a Helper Pup,' Joe said. 'But one day . . .'

He was sure Patch would pass the initial test in a few weeks' time and then he could start his proper training.

The girls played with the puppies for half an hour and finally chose the one with the pink dot on his head as he was very cuddly.

'He fell asleep in my arms!'

'We're going to call him Jasper,' they agreed as they left.

'See you in three weeks' time,' Mrs Hodges said as she and Marnie waved them goodbye.

By the time the girls and their mum had left, Patch and the other puppies were very tired and they crawled over each other to get the sleeping spot they wanted.

'Time we were going too,' Joe's mum decided. 'It's been a long day.'

'Come back whenever you like,' Mrs Hodges told Joe. 'I can see you're a natural when it comes to puppies.'

'I will,' Joe said. But he also needed to go to Lenny's classes so he could learn the correct way to look after a Helper Dog puppy. If Patch passed his initial test at forty-nine days old, he'd be coming to live with them after that. Only yesterday it had seemed like each day took ages to be over, but now Joe didn't know how he was going to fit in everything that needed to be done. It was going to be a very busy few weeks!

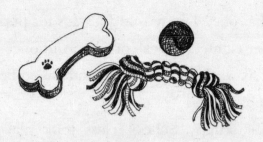

Chapter 5

The following Tuesday, Lenny asked Joe to help out with one of the regular dog classes at the centre.

'I don't just train Helper Dogs – we run a variety of classes for all sorts of dogs,' he said, handing Joe a spreadsheet. 'This is the timetable for all our classes until the end of the summer. I thought it would be a good idea for you to come along to a few to prepare for looking after Patch.' He pointed out the Puppy Pre-school class at 9.30 a.m. on Mondays. 'Once Patch has passed his initial test, he will come along to that one,' Lenny told Joe. 'It's for puppies under eighteen weeks of age. And once he's had six weeks of that, he'll graduate to Puppy School.'

The Puppy School class took place at 10.30 a.m., straight after Puppy Pre-school, and at 11.30 there was Obedience for dogs of all ages. Tuesdays were for Puppy Tumble-tots and Agility. Wednesday and Saturday mornings were taken up with Helper Dog training.

'Helper Dogs-in-training can come along to any of the other classes as well,' Lenny added.

Thursdays were for Advanced Obedience and Kennel Club Bronze, Silver and Gold training classes and exams.

'Fridays are reserved for individual sessions with dogs that need extra help, as well as Friday Flyball in the evenings,' Lenny explained.

'What's Flyball?' Joe asked.

Lenny grinned. 'It's like dog relay racing,' he said. 'They're in teams and take it in turns to race after a tennis ball that comes flying out of this.' He patted a box with a press-pad on it. 'The dog presses the pad, grabs the ball in his mouth and races back to his handler, usually over hurdles, and then it's the next dog's turn.'

'Sounds like fun.'

'Oh, it is and it gets very noisy here on Fridays with everyone shouting encouragement at their dogs and the dogs almost bursting for it to be their turn next.'

'Can all dogs do it?'

'Sure. Some breeds will be faster than others in competitions, but that doesn't matter here. What we want is for the dog and its owners to have fun – and they do.'

'Do Helper Dogs join in that class?' Joe asked.

'Not often,' Lenny said. 'They're too busy learning how to be Helper Dogs. Patch'll be too young to join in until he's a year old and he'll hopefully be living with Sam by then. Helper Dogs have approved his request.'

'What about once school starts,' asked Joe, thinking about the Helper Dogs classes. 'Maybe I could miss a bit . . . ?'

'Not to worry – our timetable changes to early evenings once term-time starts so you'll be able to bring Patch along after school, and to the Saturday morning classes, of course. But nice try,' Lenny winked.

Just before 9.30, eight puppies arrived at the training centre with their owners for the Puppy Tumble-tots session. Joe couldn't help noticing that some of the owners looked a lot like their dogs: one lady with a red setter puppy had hair that exactly matched the colour of the dog's fur. Another lady with a cross-looking expression on her face had a pug puppy that looked a bit grumpy and snapped irritably when another pup got in its way. Some of the owners smiled at Joe or rolled their eyes as their excited puppies dragged them inside, but others looked worried.

'Slow down, Noah,' a tall thin man kept telling his gangly Irish wolfhound pup as he pulled him back on his lead. 'You'll have me over again.' But Noah was too eager to join his friends to go anywhere slowly.

'The pups love this class,' Lenny grinned as Joe helped him stretch out a long fabric tunnel. 'And it helps them with their flexibility and coordination as well as concentration. I don't do any jumps or plank-walking with young pups, though, because their joints are fragile and still developing.'

Once the Tumble-tots course was laid out, it was time for the puppies and their handlers to try it.

Joe watched as the pug pup yipped its way excitedly round the course and its cross-looking owner ran alongside, issuing instructions.

'This way . . . Over there . . . No – through it . . . through it! . . . That's it . . . good dog!'

'Well done,' Lenny said, and the cross-looking lady finally smiled and her puppy stood up on its back legs and wagged its tail as she gave it a treat.

When it was Noah's turn, his owner asked if Lenny could take him round instead as he'd hurt his ankle the day before.

'Why don't you give it a go, Joe?' Lenny suggested.

Joe pointed to himself. 'Me?' he mouthed and Lenny nodded.

Joe took a deep breath.

'Here, these might help if he gets stuck in the tunnel,' Noah's owner said encouragingly, handing Joe a bag of dog treats along with Noah's lead.

'Keep Noah on the lead for now,' Lenny advised. 'If he does it well, you can try him off the lead next time.'

Joe nodded as he tried to remember which obstacle the pug puppy had started with.

Noah looked up at him, wagged his tail and then pulled Joe over to the twelve orange and blue slalom poles. Joe grinned as he was tugged along. Noah must have been watching the pug because he remembered where the course had started.

'You're a smart dog,' Joe told him, giving the wolfhound a pat. Then they were off.

Noah squeezed in between the right and then the left narrowly divided poles like slalom skiers did. It had been a lot easier for the smaller pug to get through, but Noah just about managed.

Next he picked his way over the fences that weren't actually jumps because the poles were laid on the ground.

'That's it, Noah!' Joe praised the pup, firmly holding on to the lead.

It was only when they reached the nylon tunnel that Noah faltered. He took one look at it and sat down.

'Come on, Noah – in there,' Joe said, putting down the lead and pointing at where he wanted him to go.

Noah tilted his head to one side as if he were listening to exactly what Joe was saying, but he still didn't move.

Joe ran to the other end of the tunnel and called to Noah through it. 'Come, Noah, come!'

Noah stood up and peered at Joe through the tunnel. He whined and took one step towards him. His paw was actually on the fabric, but then he took it off again. Nope, he wasn't going in there.

Joe ran back to Noah, showed him the treat bag and took out a few. Noah definitely wanted one of those.

Joe threw a handful into the tunnel and then raced round to the other end and lifted it so Noah could see all the way through to him.

Noah was already part-way into the tunnel, gobbling up his treats.

'Noah, come!'

And Noah did. Once the treats were finished, he crawled on his belly through the tunnel to Joe, who shook the treat bag as extra encouragement. The puppy emerged from the tunnel, tail wagging, and Joe gave him another treat and a hug.

'Nicely done, Noah and Joe,' Lenny said, as Noah delicately stepped in and out of three hoops laid in a row on the ground, before joining the rest of the pups.

'Patch'll love this,' Joe said to Lenny when Noah was back with his owner. He couldn't wait for Patch to be old enough to join in.

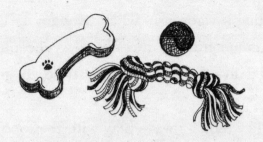

Chapter 6

As the next few weeks went by, Joe crossed off the days until Patch's initial Helper Dog test on his calendar one by one. And every day, on his way home from the training classes, Joe stopped at Mrs Hodges's house to see Patch, who always raced over to greet him with his little tail wagging.

Joe now played with Patch and the other puppies outside, mostly, as the weather was sunny. Patch and his sister liked to play with a yellow, blue and red rope toy, bracing their puppy legs for support as they tugged, and shaking it vigorously when they got it. Then the game turned into chase as the puppy who'd lost hold of the toy tried to get it back.

They didn't always play with the rope toy. They played with anything they found. One day Mrs Hodges put an empty plastic bottle in the pen and all the puppies raced around holding it. When they'd had enough of toys, there was always puppy-wrestling and chasing their own and each other's tails to be done before they fell asleep, often in mid-play.

Joe loved playing with them and watching them. Marnie usually sat beside him and watched her lively puppies too.

On the morning of the test Joe woke up really early.

Patch woke up really early too, although he didn't know that today was the most important day of his seven-week-old life so far. He had eaten his breakfast and was playing with Little

Blue when he heard the doorbell ring. He tilted his head to one side with his little black ear down.

'Hello,' Mrs Hodges said as she opened the door, closely followed by Marnie as usual. 'They've just had their breakfast and Patch is all ready for you.'

Patch sniffed the familiar smell. It was the smell of a friend, and a moment later there Joe was.

Joe crouched down beside the puppy enclosure and all the little dogs rushed over to him, but Patch was the first one to reach him.

'Hello, Patch,' he said as he lifted the puppy out of the pen and stroked him.

'Can I help with the test?' he asked Lenny, who had followed him in.

'Yes – I'll need some help,' Lenny answered. 'But make sure you don't talk to Patch while the test is happening in case it confuses him.'

'OK.'

Patch had to be somewhere he wasn't familiar with for the test, so Joe carried the puppy into the lounge and set him down on the carpeted floor.

Patch's paws hadn't felt carpet before because the kitchen was tiled and the garden was made up of paving stones and grass. He trotted back and forth on it, then sat down on it, and then lay on it and rolled over on to his back to see what that felt like.

Once Patch had had time to get used to the springiness of the carpet and to wander around the lounge for a little while, Lenny rolled a soft ball for him to follow.

'Fetch . . . fetch!' Lenny said as Patch went running after the ball, his little tail wagging. 'Bring it here now; that's it, bring it.'

Patch picked up the ball in his mouth and started to bring it to Lenny, but dropped it part way and decided to sniff at the armchair leg instead.

Joe very nearly reminded Patch about the ball, but remembered just in time that he wasn't supposed to talk to him.

'Patch!' Lenny called to the puppy. 'Patch, get it.' He pointed at the ball.

Patch looked at Lenny and then he looked at the ball – and then he ran over and pounced as if it were a mouse.

'Bring it here, bring it,' Lenny said, tapping his legs and talking in an excited voice. Patch managed to carry the ball almost the whole way before dropping it this time.

Joe only just stopped himself from cheering out loud.

Next Lenny played with a soft rabbit toy with Patch, and then said 'Give,' and gently took the toy from the puppy's mouth.

Patch let go of the toy and Lenny told Patch what a good dog he was.

'That's just what I wanted you to do,' he said.

They carried on playing and every now and again Lenny said, 'Give,' until Patch released the toy without Lenny needing to tug it.

Joe was really proud of the puppy. He was doing so well.

Then, as if he knew what Joe was thinking, Patch suddenly ran over to Joe and pushed his head into him for a stroke in a way that reminded Joe of Marnie.

'So how did Patch do?' Joe asked when the test was over.

'He did just fine,' Lenny told him.

'So does that mean . . . will Patch be . . . will he really . . . can he?'

'Yes, he'll be coming to stay with you,' Lenny told Joe as they gave each other a high five.

Mrs Hodges looked just as happy about Patch's success as Joe felt. Joe could hardly believe it. He picked Patch up and hugged him until Patch started wriggling. He wanted to play with the ball Lenny had rolled.

'I'm getting a puppy,' Joe said, half to himself, as he watched Patch.

Lenny looked over at Joe and frowned. 'Just remember he won't be with you forever. He'll be going to Sam in a few months – probably around Christmastime.'

But Joe wasn't really listening. Christmas was a long way off and he wasn't looking forward to it at all. It would be the first Christmas he'd ever had without his dad being there too. But at least now he would have Patch.

My own dog at last, he thought. Although Patch wasn't just *any* dog. Patch was one totally amazing puppy.

'You'll need to make sure your house is puppy safe and friendly before he comes to you at the weekend,' Lenny warned. 'No stray wires or cables that a puppy can chew on; no gaps in the garden fence that an inquisitive pup could squeeze through.'

'OK,' Joe said.

'And you'll need to make a bark area about a metre square in your back garden – not too far from the house,' Lenny added.

'What's that for?'

'It's where you'll be teaching Patch to go to the loo.'

'Don't dogs just go where they feel like it in the garden?' Joe's mum said, when Joe told her later. 'I've never heard of dog toilets before.'

'That's what I said,' agreed Joe. 'But Lenny told me Patch isn't going to be a pet. He'll be a working dog and he needs to go in just one area of the garden, the bark-chip area, so that it'll be easier for the disabled person to clean up after him.'

'But how are we going to teach him to do that?'

'Lenny'll go over it when he comes round, but I think we have to take Patch to the bark area whenever he needs to do a wee or a poo.

And when he does, we give him tons of praise and a treat.'

'Right,' Joe's mum said. 'It sounds like there's going to be a lot for us to learn – and a lot to do. Especially once you are back at school next month – you'll have a lot to manage. You're still sure you want to take Patch on?'

'Absolutely sure,' said Joe. He'd never been more sure of anything in his life. 'It's what Dad wanted, right?'

'Right,' agreed Mum.

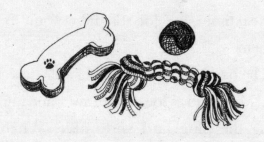

Chapter 7

The next day Joe and his mum went to the DIY superstore to buy some bark chippings.

Joe had been so busy going along to Helper Dogs every day and visiting Patch too, that although he hadn't forgotten about going back to school, he hadn't been thinking about it much, either.

But when he saw the twins and their bearded dad just ahead of him in the shop, his stomach lurched. Callum and Daniel were in his class at school; they often played football together at breaktimes, but Joe still didn't want to talk to them.

'The bark's in the gardening aisle down the end,' Mum said as Joe ducked away and hurried along the plug and wires aisle. When he reached the end, he crouched down to see if he could spot Callum and Daniel. Had they just started shopping with their dad or were they heading towards the checkout?

'No messing about in the store,' a woman wearing the shop's uniform told Joe.

'I'm not.'

But the shop assistant had already hurried past.

Joe sneaked a peek round the edge of the shelves again, but he couldn't see Callum or Daniel.

Then a hand gripped his shoulder and his blood went cold. He'd been caught. Slowly he turned round, only to find himself staring at old Mr Humphreys.

'What are you playing at?' Mr Humphreys said.

'I'm not playing, I'm trying to avoid someone,' Joe informed him.

'Who?' Mr Humphreys asked him suspiciously.

'Two boys from school.'

Mr Humphreys took a look round the end of the shelf for himself.

'Do you mean those two who are just going out of the exit with a bearded man? They look about your age.'

Joe took a careful look too. Callum and Daniel had gone!

Joe's mum came down the aisle towards them. She looked cross, but her expression changed when she saw who Joe was with.

'Hello, Mr Humphreys – fancy seeing you here,' she said.

'I'm buying some new shears,' he told her. 'It's surprising how fast hedges grow if you don't keep them trimmed. Bit like children.

Need to be watched or you won't know what trouble they'll get themselves into.' His beady eyes stared meaningfully at Joe.

'Quite,' Joe's mum said, sounding a bit confused. 'But worth all the hard work when they turn out well.'

'Hmph,' Mr Humphrey said, and he stomped off.

'Where did you get to?' Joe's mum asked as soon as Mr Humphreys had gone.

'There were kids from school here. Daniel and Callum and their dad,' he explained.

'So?'

'I didn't want to talk to them. Not about . . .' His voice trailed off. They both knew why.

His mum frowned. 'You're going to have to talk to them one day,' she said gently.

'I know. But not today.' *And not ever if he had his way.*

'Come on. I found the bark chippings.'

Once they'd bought them Joe and his mum struggled to lift the heavy bag from the trolley into the boot.

'Hope Patch appreciates all this effort,' Mum groaned.

'Hey, Joe!' a familiar voice shouted. Joe turned round. It was Charlie from his class at school. She'd got an electric wheelchair last term and now she zoomed over to them in it.

'That looks really heavy,' she said as she watched them struggling with the bag of bark chippings.

'It is,' Joe's mum replied.

'We can manage,' Joe said through gritted teeth.

'My dad'll help. He's really strong. Dad!' Charlie yelled to the man with her mum and brother.

The last thing Joe wanted was someone else's dad helping them.

'Be right there,' Charlie's dad called as he hurried towards them.

'We can manage,' Joe shouted, and he used every last ounce of strength he had to lift the bag into the back of the car.

'I see you didn't need any help after all,' Charlie's dad said when he reached them. 'You must be really strong,' he said to Joe.

'Thank you for offering to help, anyway,' Mum said.

'Joe's dad died,' Charlie told her father, and Joe thought he'd never hated anyone as much as he hated Charlie at that moment. 'He was a soldier.'

'Sorry to hear that,' Charlie's dad said as her mum and brother came to join them. 'Come on, Charlie.'

'See you at school, Joe. Can't wait to go back,' she said over her shoulder.

'I can,' Joe muttered. But Charlie didn't hear him.

When they got home, Joe set to work making a square area filled with bark chips in the back garden.

'What are you doing now, for goodness' sake?' Mr Humphreys wanted to know. He was standing on a stepladder, clipping his garden hedge with a pair of shiny new shears.

'We're getting a puppy,' Joe told him. 'He's coming on Saturday.'

'Are you indeed,' said Mr Humphreys. 'Well, just make sure you don't let it come into my garden and dig up all my plants.'

'I won't,' Joe said. What did Mr Humphreys have to be so grumpy for?

'And who's going to keep an eye on it when you're at school, I'd like to know?'

'Mum.'

'Huh, poor woman, as if she doesn't have enough on her plate at the moment from the sounds of it. I've seen that back-bedroom office light of hers on at all hours of the night. And now you expect her to look after a puppy as well.'

Joe knew his mum was doing lots of overtime, but he hadn't realized she was working late into the night.

'It's a Helper Pup,' Joe said, but Mr Humphreys wasn't listening.

'Just hope you appreciate how lucky you are to have such a good mother,' he said as Joe went back inside the house to get away from him.

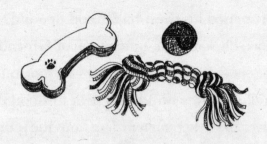

Chapter 8

The six puppies slept in a heap together, not caring who they lay on top of, or where their paws ended up. One of Patch's paws rested on top of Little Blue's head as the pair snuggled up together. It was a few days after Patch's test.

'Big day for you two,' Mrs Hodges said to the little pups, scratching the top of Patch's head as she went past to make a cup of tea. 'You'll be sleeping somewhere else tonight.'

Little Blue made a sleepy sound and stretched out her paws. Her movement woke Patch, who opened his eyes, half stood up, and then flopped back down again on top of Green Boy, who rolled on to Pink Boy, who lay half on top of Yellow Boy, who snored next to Red Girl.

Over the next quarter of an hour the puppies woke and then drifted back to sleep again. But they were all wide awake by the time Mrs Hodges started to scoop their puppy kibble into the feeding tin. Their little noses sniffed the scent of breakfast and they stumbled over each other in their haste to get to the food.

'OK now . . . wait a minute . . . all right then . . . here it is. There's enough for everyone,' Mrs Hodges said as the puppies jostled each other, trying to feed from the same spot in the tin that she placed in the centre of the puppy pen.

Mrs Hodges lifted Pink Boy and moved him to the other side of the tin. Then she moved Red Girl to a different spot so she could get to the food more easily.

The puppies had finished their breakfast and were playing together while Mrs Hodges sipped a much-needed cup of tea when the doorbell rang.

Patch immediately stopped playing and looked up.

'I bet I know who this is,' Mrs Hodges said as she got up from her armchair and headed to the front door, closely followed by Marnie.

As soon as she'd left the room, Little Blue clamped her tiny teeth on Patch's tail. He spun round in surprise and the two of them were soon playing a game of tail chase.

Mrs Hodges found Joe standing at the front door.

'Hope I'm not too early,' he mumbled, although he knew he was much earlier than the nine o'clock they'd agreed on. 'Lenny said he'd meet us here.'

'Come in, come in,' she said as Marnie wagged her tail. 'Patch will be delighted to see you.'

'Are all the puppies going to their new homes today?' Joe asked as he came inside.

'Not all of them today, but they'll all be gone by the end of the weekend,' Mrs Hodges said. 'Green Boy's off at eleven o'clock, and Mr and Mrs Royston are coming for Little Blue this afternoon. Then the Pink Boy, who they're going to call Jasper, and Red Girl are going together tomorrow morning and Yellow Boy's off after lunch.'

'Won't you miss them?' Joe asked. He didn't think he'd ever want to let the puppies go if they were his. 'And won't Marnie miss them too?' The puppies were her children after all. Joe gave Marnie a stroke.

'Marnie's had enough of them bothering her and they're old enough to go out into the world now, although I would have liked to have kept one of them,' Mrs Hodges said, leading Joe into the kitchen. 'But they're all going to good homes.'

'Hello, Patch,' Joe said as Patch ran over to him, ready to be scooped up in Joe's arms.

Half an hour later the doorbell rang again and Lenny came in.

'Today's the big day,' he said, heading over to Joe, who was playing with Patch and the other puppies.

'He'll probably cry the first night he's with you, but don't worry,' Mrs Hodges told Joe. 'Put this with him and it should help.'

She gave Joe a small square of dirty-looking yellow blanket and saw his confused look.

'It's a small piece of the blanket from the puppy pen that has the scent of his mum and his brothers and sisters on it,' she told him. 'I've cut it up so they can each take a little bit of it with them.' She picked up one of the six soft star toys that were also in the pen. 'All the puppies have got one of these to take with them too. They're all stars as far as I'm concerned,' she added.

Joe nodded.

Mrs Hodges blew her nose and headed over to the kitchen counter. She picked up one of six small bags of puppy food.

'This is what he's been used to eating,' she explained.

'You'll need to introduce the Helper Dog puppy food gradually to this bag,' Lenny told Joe. 'Begin with two thirds of this one that Patch is used to and one third of the Helper Dogs puppy food and in a few days make it half and half, then two thirds and a third, until finally you make it all Helper Dogs puppy food.'

Joe nodded again. There were so many things to remember and he desperately wanted to get it all right. He'd read through the Helper Pup manual Lenny had given him three times already.

He followed Lenny with Patch in his arms, and at the front door Mrs Hodges gave the dog a last hug.

'I'm going to miss you,' she told him.

Patch licked her face with his little pink tongue as if he were saying goodbye.

'You can come and see him whenever you like,' Joe reassured her.

'Thank you,' Mrs Hodges smiled.

Lenny pulled open the doors at the back of his Helper Dogs van. Inside was a metal puppy crate with a blanket and a soft rabbit toy waiting for Patch inside it.

It's a cage, Joe thought. He didn't want to put Patch in a cage, not even for the short journey to his street.

'Can't I just hold him on my lap?' he asked Lenny.

Lenny shook his head. 'He'll be safer in there,' he said, pulling open the crate door.

Joe put Patch inside the crate and then swallowed hard as Patch looked out at him and whimpered.

'He doesn't like being in there,' Joe protested.

'He'll get used to it,' Lenny told him. 'Lots of dogs come to love them. They're like the dog's kennel. A special room of his own.'

Patch didn't like the smell of the crate or the hard shiny bars that hurt his puppy teeth when he tried to bite them. Then, even worse, the crate began to shake as the engine started up. Patch was terrified of the loud roaring sound. He shook with fear and panted as the car drove off.

'It's all right, Patch,' Joe said softly. 'Nearly there.'

It was the first time Patch had been away from his mum, and his brothers and sisters, and the first time he'd been in a car – and he didn't like it one little bit. He whined and cried and panted the whole way to show what he thought of being in a cage inside a roaring beast.

Finally the van stopped and the back doors opened. The darkness of the van interior was replaced by sunlight and fresh air from outside.

Patch put his paw to the crate bars and looked straight at Joe and Lenny. There was no mistaking what he was trying to say.

'He can come out now,' Lenny said, and Joe opened the crate door and lifted Patch out. The puppy's heart was beating very fast and Joe did his best to soothe him.

'All Helper Dog pups have to get used to going in cars,' Lenny said. 'It's part of their training. Going on buses and trains too.'

Joe's mum was waiting for them at the door.

'Best to keep him in the one room to start with,' Lenny said to them both as Joe set Patch down on the lounge floor. 'Letting him wander all over the place might be a bit overwhelming for him.'

Joe hadn't thought of that. He wanted to be able to show Patch the garden and take him upstairs to his bedroom where they'd decided Patch would sleep at first.

'And get him used to going in that crate at night-time. The Helper Dogs people issue them because they don't want to be charged for any damage a pup might do. Once he's toilet-trained he can sleep downstairs,' Lenny told Joe.

But Joe didn't want Patch to sleep downstairs all alone. He was sure that whoever Patch went to live with eventually would want him to sleep in their room too.

'Patch wouldn't do any damage,' he said.

'Not on purpose, no,' agreed Lenny. 'But to a pup, the wire to your TV is an interesting wiggly snake toy to chew on – especially when he starts teething and is looking for something to bite. He won't know slippers aren't toys, or socks, and puppy teeth are sharp. Shredded cushions and the like can all be avoided if you put a puppy in his crate when you can't watch him.'

Joe looked down at Patch. He was sure the puppy wasn't a cushion shredder.

'We'll keep a good eye on him,' Joe's mum said.

'Well, don't say you haven't been warned,' said Lenny, smiling and handing Joe a very soft collar for Patch. 'Put this on him and then just leave it,' he told Joe. 'In no time at all he'll get used to it and not be bothered.'

But Patch didn't want the collar on and he scratched at it the minute it was clipped on. Joe picked up the star toy Mrs Hodges had given the pup and wiggled it about on the floor.

'Here, Patch – what's this?'

Patch was immediately interested and forgot all about the collar as he tried to pounce on the star, his little puppy tail wagging.

'You'll need to keep a diary of what Patch does, and every month there's a form to fill in to show how he's progressing. You can do it all online on our Helper Dogs website.'

'What about photos?' Joe asked as Patch chewed on the star and made little growling sounds. 'Should I take some photos of Patch for his diary and progress form?'

'Joe's got his dad's camera,' Mum said.

'It takes really good pictures,' Joe told Lenny, 'and it can do videos too.'

'Pictures and videos would be great,' Lenny said. 'I bet Sam'll love to see them.'

Patch was so small at the moment it was hard to imagine that one day he'd be an assistance dog.

They all looked at the puppy determinedly dragging the star toy across the floor.

'Right, I better get on.' Lenny turned to Joe. 'I know you're going to do a brilliant job with Patch.' He knelt down and gave Patch a final tickle behind one ear. 'I'll see you both very soon.'

Joe suddenly felt nervous. This was it. Patch was his responsibility now and it was a big one.

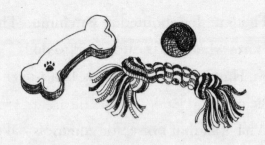

Chapter 9

Once Lenny had gone, Joe's mum went back to work in her office and Joe took Patch out into their small garden. Patch explored the flower beds, but didn't go too far away.

Joe was thinking about his dad. 'You'd have liked him,' he told Patch. 'You'd have liked my dad very much.'

He threw the soft yellow ball he'd bought for Patch a short distance across the lawn.

Patch watched it land, looked up at Joe, looked back at the ball and then made a yipping sound as he ran over to retrieve it.

'That's it!' Joe shouted as Patch ran. 'That's it! That's what you're supposed to do.'

Mr Humphreys poked his head over the hedge.

'What's all that noise, for goodness' sake?'

Then he saw Patch.

'All that yipping and yapping racket,' he complained as Patch wagged his tail at him. 'I hope he isn't going to be barking all the time and giving me a headache. Looks like he'll be a little imp. What's wrong with his ear?'

'Nothing,' Joe replied. 'There's nothing wrong with him at all. He's just perfect.'

'We'll see about that,' Mr Humphreys said doubtfully as Joe took Patch back inside.

Once the puppy had had another drink of water from his bowl he looked up at Joe and his little tail wagged. He was ready to play again!

Joe put his hand in the bag of puppy toys he and his mum had bought at the pet store and squeaked one of them. Patch was so excited by the sound that he tried to get into the bag to see what was in there.

'Wait a minute,' Joe laughed, and he pulled a colourful patchwork snake toy, which was soft-quilted and squeaked, from the bag, shook it and then threw it a little way across the room. 'Here it is; go get it, get Squeaker!'

Patch raced after the patchwork snake, stopped and put out his paw to touch it. When the toy moved, he hopped back, then put his paw out again. This time it didn't move or squeak and he pounced, shook it and dragged it back to Joe.

Joe laughed and laughed because Patch looked so funny carrying the snake, which was almost twice as long as him. It was the first time he'd laughed – really laughed – since they'd heard the news about his dad. The laughter sounded strange to his ears, but once he started he couldn't stop. He laughed until tears ran down his face.

Upstairs in her spare-bedroom office, Joe's mum smiled as she brushed away her own tears.

Patch dropped the toy in Joe's lap and then half sat and half slumped on the carpet.

Lenny had said puppies had a special way of sitting. *It's like they can't be bothered to sit up properly.* Now Joe was seeing the 'puppy sit' for himself.

'Give, Patch, give,' Joe said as he tugged a little harder, but not too hard.

Patch immediately let go of the toy.

'Good dog,' Joe said, and he held the snake out to the puppy so they could carry on with their tugging game.

Patch's little tail stuck straight up as he held on to the snake and made soft play-growling sounds. He was totally engrossed in the game one moment and utterly exhausted the next. A second later Patch flopped down on his side and fell fast asleep.

'Well, it has been a very busy morning for you,' Joe murmured as he watched the little puppy sleeping. He wasn't sure if he'd wake Patch up by moving, so he stayed where he was, just watching him. But, as the seconds and then the minutes on the wall clock ticked past and Patch still didn't stir, Joe decided to risk going upstairs to grab his dad's camera. He stood up as quietly as he could and kept looking over at Patch as he went up the stairs, but the puppy didn't move.

Joe picked up the camera and came back downstairs with it.

His dad had loved taking photographs and he'd shown Joe how to take good pictures by making sure his subject wasn't in the absolute centre of the frame and that the sun wasn't too bright. *Don't want the shadows of your feet in the picture too, do you?* his dad had said.

Like a ghost? Joe had laughed.

It had seemed so funny at the time, but not any more.

'Do you want me to look after him for a while to give you a break?' Joe's mum whispered when she came downstairs at lunchtime and saw Patch lying on the carpet, still fast asleep.

Joe shook his head. 'I don't need a break,' he whispered back as he followed his mum to the kitchen for a sandwich. He was having too much fun spending the day with Patch to need a break.

A quarter of an hour later Patch made a sleepy little sound, stretched out his paws, yawned and opened his eyes.

'Hello, Patch,' Joe said, and Patch crawled into his lap for a stroke. Whenever the little pup snuggled up to him, Joe could hardly believe how soft his fur was.

A few minutes later Joe took his first photo of Patch having a long drink of water from his bowl. Then they both ran out to the bark area so Patch could do his business.

'That's it . . . This way, Patch, over here . . . good dog,' he said.

Once he'd finished, Patch scampered over to the flowers round the edge of the lawn and Joe took lots of pictures of the puppy sniffing at them. But he wasn't quite quick enough to capture the moment that Patch sneezed after he'd sniffed the rosemary bush Joe's mum had planted only the week before. *It's the herb of remembrance*, she'd said.

'That would have been an excellent shot, an award-winning shot,' Joe told the puppy.

Patch ran across the lawn towards the hedge and next-door's garden. Behind the foliage Joe could hear Mr Humphreys whistling and the sound of water spraying from the hosepipe. The gardens in Joe's road weren't very big and in no time Patch had disappeared through the hedge.

'No, Patch – come back!' Joe called frantically as he ran after the dog.

But Patch had seen the long, twirling green snake with water gushing out of it and he raced towards it, yipping his high puppy bark.

Mr Humphreys hadn't noticed Patch squeeze through the hedge or heard him yipping. 'What!' he cried in surprise as the puppy raced through his legs. 'Get out of it!' He dropped the hosepipe as he slipped backwards and toppled on to the wet grass.

Now the hosepipe became even more exciting as it took on a wild life of its own. Patch's little tail wagged and he yipped with delight as the water splashed around. He raced into the spray so he could get thoroughly soaked.

Joe clambered over the back wall into Mr Humphreys' garden.

'I'm so sorry!' he shouted as he ran to help his neighbour up. Patch rolled over in a puddle of water that the hose had left, totally in his element.

'Get that puppy back to its own garden!' Mr Humphreys yelled furiously. He was soaked to the skin, and covered in mud and grass stains too. He looked over to see where Patch had got through. 'That needs to be repaired.'

'I'll do it straight away,' Joe said.

'No, *I'll* do it,' Mr Humphreys said crossly. 'I'll do a better job than you and I don't want him getting through again.'

Joe picked a soggy Patch up and took him back to their own garden and inside the house, where he dried him with kitchen towels. The dog yawned. He was tired after all the excitement and was soon sleeping again.

'Little puppies need a lot of sleep,' Joe's mum said when she came down from her office a few minutes later to make a cup of tea.

'Especially little puppies who've been in next-door's garden and showered by the hosepipe,' Joe added, and he told her what had happened.

'Lucky Mr Humphreys wasn't hurt,' Joe's mum remarked drily, and Joe grinned and nodded.

'Just got a bit muddy,' he said.

While Patch twitched as he dreamt his puppy dreams, Joe sat down at the computer and wrote his first entry in Patch's diary. He thought about the soldier called Sam that Patch would one day be going to live with and wondered what he might like to hear about.

Suddenly he had an idea. Because it was called Patch's diary he decided to write it as if Patch himself were telling Sam what he'd been up to.

Today I came to live at my new house with Joe and his mum and Squeaker. Squeaker's a toy snake and twice as big as me, but I'm much stronger . . .

Joe added a photo of Patch holding Squeaker. Then he remembered the Mr Humphreys adventure.

I also got to visit a very nice garden next door. Mr Humphreys has a snake called Hose that sprayed water everywhere. I loved playing with Hose, but Mr Humphreys fell over and got all muddy and a bit cross. He says he doesn't want me in his garden EVER again, but I know he doesn't mean it!

Joe grinned at the memory.

I think I'm going to like it here. Joe and his mum give me lots of cuddles and nice things to eat, but there're still lots of things for me to learn before I can become a proper Helper Dog. ☺

Joe pressed SAVE and then went to see what was for dinner.

Far away a nurse helped Sam to hold his iPad to look at Patch's first diary entry.

'What a sweet-looking puppy,' she commented.

'It's a Helper Pup and his name's Patch,' Sam told her. 'I'm hoping one day he can be my pup.'

Now he had a goal to strive for.

'If I can get well enough to leave the hospital, I'll be moved to a specially adapted ground-floor flat where Patch can come and live with me,' Sam explained.

It wasn't going to be easy, but he was determined to be strong enough to do so by Christmas. If he didn't make it by then, Patch would probably be given to another soldier and he knew as soon as he saw Patch's picture that he wanted the puppy to be his Helper Dog more than anything else in the world.

'Well then, we'll have to make sure you're fit enough,' the nurse said, pretending not to notice the pain on Sam's face as he tried to move. The soldier had a long way to go yet.

'I have to be,' he said.

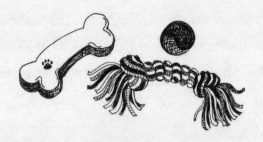

Chapter 10

In the evening Joe's mum carried Patch's crate up the stairs and Joe carried Patch up.

'You're sure you want him in your room and you don't mind getting up to let him do his business in the garden in the middle of the night?' she asked.

'Sure,' said Joe firmly.

'It might be three or four times.'

'I'm sure.'

So Mum put the puppy crate next to Joe's bed and went to fill Patch's night-time water bowl.

'I'm very proud of you,' she said as she gave Joe a kiss on the forehead and Patch a last stroke. 'If you need any help, just give me a yell.'

'OK.'

'See you in the morning then.' She put the water bowl next to the crate and pulled the door to.

'Night, Mum.'

Joe yawned and opened the crate door. The piece of yellow blanket was still inside it along with the star toy.

'In you go, Patch.'

But Patch didn't want to go in the crate and he headed off in the other direction towards Joe's curtains.

'Come on, you have to go into the crate.'

Patch sat down in a puppy slump and looked at Joe with his head to one side. Joe smiled. He could see by his sleepy look that Patch wasn't going to be able to stay awake for much longer, but he wasn't going to go back in that crate, either.

'Just a little bit more playing then,' Joe said, and he rolled a soft ball across the bedroom rug for Patch to run after. Patch's runs soon slowed to walks and then staggers, and the sleepy pup finally lay down next to the ball.

Once Joe was sure he was fast asleep, he lifted Patch into the crate and pushed the door to before crawling into bed himself.

He'd been asleep for a few hours when he heard a crying sound and was instantly awake.

'It's all right,' Joe murmured into the darkness. For a second he thought Patch was crying because he missed his mum, and his brothers and sisters, in the same way that Joe missed his dad. But then he remembered Patch probably needed to go for a wee – and little puppies couldn't wait for long. 'OK, OK!'

He picked Patch up and headed down the stairs and out into the garden to the bark area. It was a beautiful night and the stars were so bright that it wasn't even dark.

Joe watched Patch as he stalked one of his new toys, a brown woolly dog, and then ran at it and pounced. Then he stalked the dustpan brush, which was too heavy for him to pick up, but he managed to drag it along by its bristles, making little growling sounds as he did so.

'Time to go back now,' Joe yawned.

Patch didn't seem to be sleepy at all and wanted to carry on playing with the brush, even if it was the middle of the night.

'Come on, Patch.'

Finally Joe had to pick the puppy up and carry him back to his bedroom. He was about to put Patch back in the crate, but when the puppy whimpered he just couldn't bring himself to do it.

'You can sleep on the floor,' Joe said, pulling the bedding out from the bottom of the crate.

But Patch didn't want to sleep on the floor either. He stood on his back legs and tried to get into Joe's bed, whining to come up until Joe lifted him on to the bed.

'Just don't have any accidents,' he told the puppy as they fell asleep cuddled up together.

Joe woke up to find Patch's little tongue licking his face. He smiled and then looked down at the bottom of his bed and frowned.

'Uh-oh.'

Mum found him stuffing his wet quilt into the washing machine while Patch played with a sock that had fallen from the washing basket. Fortunately Patch was only a small puppy and so the mess he'd made on Joe's bed wasn't too bad.

'Sorry —' Joe started to say.

But his mum just smiled and shrugged. 'It's what happens when you have a baby animal in the house,' she said.

'Are you pleased he's here?' Joe asked her as she took Patch's food down from the shelf.

'Very pleased. You're doing a good job with him, Joe. A very good job. Your dad would be proud of you.' She smiled.

'I wish he could've met Patch.'

'Me too.'

Joe shook some of the food Mrs Hodges had given them into Patch's bowl and then added some of the Helper Dogs puppy food to it.

'Here you go, little pup,' he said, putting it in front of the dog.

Patch immediately dropped the sock, put his head down and gobbled it all up.

'Mrs Hodges said puppies are always hungry,' Joe told his mum.

'Looks like she's right.'

'I hope all of Marnie's puppies are having as nice a time as Patch is,' Joe said as Patch licked his bowl until it shone.

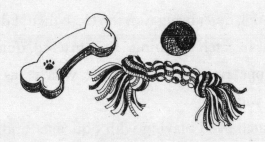

Chapter 11

Patch saw Mr Humphreys up the ladder in the garden and ran over to him, yipping excitedly.

'When's he going to get properly trained?' Mr Humphreys said.

'He's too young even to go to puppy classes,' Joe told him. 'Besides, Patch isn't really allowed out of our house and garden yet because he hasn't been fully vaccinated. He's having the rest of his inoculations at the end of this week, so for the moment we just spend all day, every day together, playing.' Joe smiled, but Mr Humphreys looked alarmed.

'Well, don't bring him too close then, I don't want to catch anything,' he muttered, quickly disappearing down his ladder, which was just fine with Joe.

Patch liked playing with Squeaker and the ball Joe had bought him, but he also turned almost anything into a toy to be played with – a cardboard box one day, a cushion the next. A plastic bottle made a nice rattly sound and so did a crisp packet. And there was always his own tail to chase.

One afternoon, Joe tried to teach Patch to sit as he'd seen the other dogs do at the classes Lenny ran.

'Sit, Patch, sit,' he instructed.

Patch looked up at him with his head on one side, not at all sure what Joe wanted him to do.

'Sit,' Joe repeated, and he squatted as if he were about to sit. But Patch still didn't do as he asked.

Joe sat down on the floor and Patch jumped on to his lap and licked his face. Joe sighed, gently put Patch back on the ground and stood up. Maybe teaching Patch wasn't going to be so easy after all.

Patch looked up at Joe and then he sat down.

'That's it! Yes! Sit!' Joe shouted. 'Good dog!'

'You OK, Joe?' Mum called from upstairs.

'Yes, I'm just teaching Patch to sit,' he called back up to her.

Patch pounced on Squeaker and dragged the snake over to Joe for a game.

'Sit,' Joe said, after they'd been playing for a little while, and he lifted his arm like a pendulum up to his chest.

Patch wagged his tail, unsure what to do.

'Sit,' Joe said, repeating the gesture, and Patch sat.

'Yes!' Joe cried. 'Yes, yes, yes!' and he ran into the kitchen to get Patch a puppy treat and Patch ran after him, very excited too.

In the days that followed, Patch learnt to 'sit', then Joe taught him to 'wait' and held up his hand in a 'stop' gesture to show the puppy what he meant. Patch was very eager to learn, especially when there were tasty treats involved.

'He's so smart, Mum,' Joe told her a few days later over lunch. 'Look what he can do now.'

Having already taught Patch to sit and stand, and also to wait and come when he was called, Joe had now taught him something new.

'Get your lead, Patch, get your lead,' Joe said, pointing in the appropriate direction.

Patch trotted over to his lead, which lay like a snake on the floor, picked it up in his mouth and brought it back to Joe.

'Yay, well done, Patch!'

'He really is a fast learner,' said Joe's mum. She crouched down and Patch ran into her arms to be stroked. He knew he'd done well.

At the end of the week Lenny came round to see how they were all getting on and to take Joe and Patch to the vet.

Before they left, Joe showed him the photos he'd taken.

'There he is in the garden with Squeaker, his favourite toy . . . and there he is sleeping. It's funny when he snores.'

Lenny was really impressed. 'And you've added these to his diary?' he asked.

'Yes, but I wasn't sure how many photos I could put in the diary,' Joe told him. 'How many do you think would be OK?'

'All of them,' said Lenny. 'If I was Sam, there could never be too many.'

'Right,' said Joe. If he was Sam, he'd want to see them all too.

'I think Head Office are going to be very interested in seeing this diary too,' added Lenny.

'What else can I teach Patch? He's so clever and he loves learning.'

'That's because you're making his learning fun,' Lenny explained, giving Patch a hug. 'You've got a natural-born dog trainer for a son, Mary.'

Joe blushed.

'He does seem to have a way with him,' Mum agreed.

'You've made a fine start to Patch's Helper Dog training,' said Lenny. 'And he'll be well ahead of all the others at pre-puppy class.'

Lenny drove Joe and Patch to the vet's in the Helper Dogs van as Joe's mum had a meeting.

'Who's this then?' the receptionist asked as she came out from behind her desk to say hello to Lenny.

'This is Patch.'

'What a sweetie. How's Riley doing?' the receptionist enquired.

'Getting there slowly,' Lenny told her.

'Who's Riley?' asked Joe when they sat down with Patch to wait for the vet.

'A dog I've been seeing. He's refused to go out of the house ever since he was attacked by another dog,' Lenny said as Patch investigated his shoes and pulled at the Velcro straps.

Joe gulped. What if Patch got attacked?

'Does that often happen?' he asked.

Lenny shook his head. 'No. You and Patch have nothing to worry about.'

But Joe couldn't help worrying. He didn't ever want Patch to be hurt or unhappy.

A few minutes later the vet called them into the consulting room.

'What a fine-looking puppy,' she said, listening to Patch's heart through her stethoscope.

Patch gave an *ouch* yelp when he had his vaccination, but the pain was soon forgotten when the vet gave him a puppy treat.

'I'll just scan his microchip to make sure that's working fine,' she said, and waved a machine that looked a bit like a barcode reader across the nape of Patch's neck and then looked at the screen. 'That's all good.'

'What's he need a microchip for?' Joe asked.

'So that if Patch ever got lost and was handed in to the police or a vet's or even an animal shelter, they'd be able to find out who he belonged to and return him to his owner,' the vet explained as she saw them out.

'Not long now and you'll be able to take Patch for a proper walk, but before that the two of you can start coming along to some classes at the training centre,' Lenny said when he dropped Joe and Patch off at home.

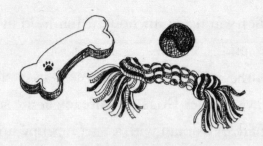

Chapter 12

On Monday morning Joe's mum dropped him and Patch off at the Helper Dogs centre for their first pre-puppy class.

'I wish I could come with you,' she said. 'But we're so busy at work.'

'It's OK, Mum,' Joe said. He knew she was doing her best.

He opened the hatchback boot and then the door of Patch's puppy crate in the back. Patch was so pleased to see Joe that he almost jumped out of the crate, his tail wagging, ready for their next adventure.

'Pick you up in an hour,' Mum said as she drove off.

There were three other cars as well as Lenny's Helper Dogs van already in the small car park. A woman with a Staffie puppy smiled as she passed Joe and Patch and headed into the training centre. The two puppies were wildly desperate to say hello to each other, their tails wagging as they stretched their leads as far as they would go.

Then a brown and white spaniel arrived and Patch wanted to say hello to her too.

'Come on, Patch,' Joe said, coaxing him into the centre.

'Puppy playtime's out the back,' Lenny told the puppies as they arrived with their owners. There were four puppies already playing together in the outside bark-covered area at the back of the training centre.

Joe unclipped Patch's lead and he raced to join a wire-haired terrier and mixed collie dog as well as the pug and spaniel. The puppies sniffed and wagged their tails, chased, jumped and rolled over each other.

Soon three more arrived. Some of them were shy and hovered close to their owners' legs rather than playing, but Patch wasn't shy at all.

'He thinks everyone wants to be his friend,' Joe said to Lenny.

'And they do,' Lenny smiled as he watched Patch and the others playing. Then he raised his voice so everyone could hear. 'Right! Call your puppies back to you now.'

'Toby . . . Kai . . . Lulu . . . Jellybean . . . Otis . . . Dex . . . Harvey . . .' The owners called to their puppies. A few of the dogs listened, but most of them were too busy playing to hear.

'Here, Patch . . . Patch, come!' Joe called, and Patch immediately came running back to him. All their *pre*-pre-puppy training had been worth it and Joe felt very proud of Patch. He clipped Patch's lead to his collar and gave him a small biscuit for being so good as they waited for the other owners to grab their pups.

Once the puppies had all been retrieved, Lenny led everyone inside and asked them to form a circle and introduce themselves and their puppies. All the other owners were grown-ups and Joe felt a bit nervous. Some of the people took ages to tell everyone all about their pup, but Joe didn't.

'I'm Joe and this is Patch and he's a Helper Pup,' he said.

'Joe's looking after him for us,' Lenny said. 'And he's doing a very fine job.'

One of the first things puppies in the class needed to learn was not to eat something they weren't supposed to.

'It's very important for your pups to understand that sometimes they can't have something until you say they can,' Lenny said. 'What if you dropped a bottle of pills on the floor? Pills that might look a lot like treats to a puppy. Especially a puppy who doesn't usually stop to think before he eats. Anyone have a puppy like that?'

Most of the puppy owners, including Joe, put their hands up. Patch had tried to eat a chocolate biscuit from a plate the other day and Joe had only just got to it in time. Chocolate was very bad for dogs.

'Puppies get very hungry and you don't want yours to get sick by eating something he shouldn't. So today we're going to practise the "leave it" command with lots of tasty foods that your puppy would probably like to have very much. He'll find it hard to understand why he can't have the treats straight away, but he, or she, has to learn that they need to listen to you.'

Lenny gave everyone a treat or two and told them to hold it in their hands and show it to their puppy.

Joe showed Patch the treat in his hand, but when Patch jumped up at him, he closed his hand and said 'Leave!' just as he had been told. He felt a bit mean, but the puppies had to learn not to eat just *anything* – and it was especially important for a Helper Pup.

Patch sat down and looked up at Joe, his head tilted to one side as if he were trying to work out what was going on. He looked around at the other people and their puppies, all doing the same thing. Then he looked back at Joe.

Joe showed him the treat in his hand again and this time Patch sat still and didn't try to grab it.

'Leave it,' Joe said.

Patch didn't try to get the treat, but his eyes never left the hand that Joe had the treat in.

After a few more tries Lenny said, 'OK, they've all done very well – you can give the puppies the treats now.'

Joe held the treat out to Patch, who stood up and took it gently from him and gobbled it up as fast as he could. Joe couldn't help laughing.

'Right, that's enough keeping still,' Lenny said. 'Now we're going to learn how to walk a dog.'

The puppy owners looked at each other.

'But we know how to do that,' the woman with the pug puppy called Toby pointed out.

'Everyone knows how to,' said Jellybean's dad.

Lenny shook his head. 'Everyone knows how to drag or be dragged along by a dog. But most people don't know how to make sure a dog walks on a loose lead politely, and stops and sits down when it comes to a kerb.'

'How do you get a dog to do that?' the Staffie lady asked.

'By not dragging it about in the first place so it gets the idea that that's what it's supposed to do. All a dog gets from being dragged is a muscular neck!' Lenny said. 'Come on, Patch, let's show them how it's done.'

Lenny took Patch from Joe and as Patch looked up at him he said, 'I want you to try walking your puppy with the lead loose, not stretched tight, and talk to him. *That's it, Patch, this way. What's this?* The puppy should want to be with you, not racing ahead of you to see what's more interesting round the corner!'

Joe laughed and did his best to relax as he took hold of Patch's lead from Lenny.

'You'll also need to be prepared for letting your dog off his lead,' continued Lenny.

'What if Patch runs away when I let him off?' Joe said.

Lenny shook his head. 'It won't happen. People so often worry about letting their puppies off the lead, but the truth is, the longer they leave it and the older the puppy gets, the greater the risk that he *will* run away when he's finally let off. At the moment all Patch and the other puppies want is to be with you. They're not going to run away when you let them off their leads, they're going to stay close.'

Joe nodded, although he was still a little unsure. The other puppy owners looked a bit worried too.

Next Lenny dragged a wooden gate on a stand into the middle of the room.

'It's important for your puppies to learn good manners,' he said. 'And that means not barging their way in front of you when you're out and about. That's what we're going to be using this gate for. It's part of the Kennel Club's bronze exam. Your puppies aren't ready for exams yet, but they're not too young to learn to be polite.'

'What do we have to do?' Joe asked, looking down at Patch, who was sitting next to him, watching Lenny as if he were listening to his every word.

'You come to the gate with the puppy,' Lenny said, 'and then you tell him to sit as you open the gate and walk through. Then tell Patch to come through and sit and wait as you close it. Give it a try.'

Joe nodded and walked over to the gate. He could feel the eyes of all the other puppy owners staring at him.

'Sit, Patch,' he said softly.

Patch sat down and looked up at him with his head cocked on one side.

'Wait,' Joe instructed, and he held up the palm of his hand towards Patch. Then Joe opened the gate and walked through, holding it open for the puppy. 'Come, Patch.' Patch immediately jumped up and came through the gate too. 'Sit,' Joe said, and Patch sat as Joe closed the gate.

'Well done!' said Lenny. 'That was perfect. Give Patch lots of praise for being such a good puppy. Puppies and older dogs want to know that they're making you happy and so you should let them know what you like. I always think it's amazing how dogs are able to work out what we want them to do. I don't think we'd find it so easy if the roles were reversed!'

Toby the Staffie and his owner tried it next, only Toby kept jumping up as soon as she'd told him to sit down.

'You made it look so easy!' she said to Joe.

'You'll get there,' Lenny said encouragingly. But none of the other puppies managed the gate task as well as Joe and Patch.

As soon as Jellybean's dad opened the gate, Jellybean raced through it ahead of him.

'Give it another go,' Lenny said.

Jellybean's dad did, and it was better, although Jellybean still looked like she wanted to go first.

Just before the end of the class, Lenny set up a line of cones and asked Joe to unclip Patch's lead and weave in and out of them. Joe did so and Patch followed as closely behind him as he was able.

'See how close Patch is staying to Joe? That's what it'll be like for all of you on your first off-lead walk,' Lenny said. 'Puppies like to stay close.'

'Patch is a lot better behaved than Jellybean,' Jellybean's dad said doubtfully.

'I can't believe you've never had a dog before, Joe,' said Toby's mum. 'You must be a natural.'

Joe and Patch were both exhausted by the end of the class and so were the other puppies and their owners.

'Everyone's done brilliantly today. I want to hear all about your first off-lead walks with your puppies next week,' said Lenny.

'How was it?' Joe's mum asked when she came to pick him up.

'Patch did really well,' Joe said as he lifted the sleepy pup into the crate. For once Patch didn't protest. 'Lenny says it's time for Patch to have his first off-lead walk.'

'Looks like he'll need a bit of a rest first,' Mum said, laughing at Patch, who had already fallen into a deep sleep.

Patch slept for two solid hours as his little puppy brain digested all he'd learnt that morning. Joe watched him sleep. Patch was still so small and vulnerable. Was he really ready to meet other dogs and go out into the big wide world?

Once Patch woke up again he was full of energy. Joe gave him some food and an hour later he put some of Patch's favourite treats in his pocket.

Patch wagged his tail when he saw his lead. He already understood that this meant going out. Joe clipped Patch's lead to his collar and together they walked to the park at the end of the road.

'Good boy, Patch,' Joe said, once they were inside the gates. Although he tried not to show it, he was feeling very nervous as he unclipped the puppy's lead and stood up. Patch stared at him, then trotted round in a little circle and did his business.

'This way,' Joe said when Patch had finished, and he carried on walking, pretending that he didn't care if Patch came with him or not; he was going this way and Patch had better follow, just like Lenny had told them to do at the pre-puppy class.

Patch tried to keep up, but there were so many interesting smells that he kept getting distracted and stopping for a quick sniff before running to catch up with Joe again. The puppy never once let Joe out of his sight, though, and Joe, although he pretended not to, watched Patch like a hawk.

There was only one other person and their dog in the park. Joe was glad that the dog was on a lead and far away.

When they came to the big field, Joe took a ball from his pocket and threw it, but

Patch didn't want to play ball today. He didn't want to venture too far away from Joe and he wanted to sniff all the amazing new smells.

The ten minutes that a ten-week-old puppy should be walked for sped past in no time.

'Eleven minutes next week,' Joe told Patch as he re-clipped his lead. 'And then twelve minutes once you're twelve weeks old.'

Patch didn't look like he was tired at all, but when they got home Patch whimpered and bit at his paws and then he cried.

'What is it?' Joe asked desperately as his mum inspected Patch's paws to see if he had a thorn in them.

'I can't see anything,' she said, now very worried. 'Do you think he could have been stung by something?'

'I know what it is!' Joe said suddenly.

He ran out into the garden and wrenched up a few dock leaves. He'd intended to clear them away, but maybe it'd be better if he left them here for emergencies now.

Mr Humphreys poked his head over the hedge. 'Wretched weeds get everywhere,' he grumbled.

'Patch got stung by some stinging nettles,' Joe told him. 'Puppies' paws are very sensitive.'

'So what are you doing out here?'

'Getting some dock leaves,' Joe explained as he rubbed the leaves between his fingers to turn them into a pulp.

'Smart lad,' Mr Humphreys remarked as Joe ran back inside.

Joe rubbed the dock-leaf mush on Patch's paws and he stopped whimpering. The leaves really seemed to help. The little puppy crawled into Joe's lap and he cradled him.

'All right, little pup. You're all right now,' Joe said, stroking Patch's soft fur.

'But how did you know it might be stinging nettles?' Mum asked him.

'It's in the Helper Dogs training manual,' Joe told her. All that reading had been worth it to help Patch.

Later Joe switched on the computer and wrote up Patch's online diary.

Today I learnt how to wait for Joe to go first at my pre-puppy class. He says it's important because it might stop me from running into the road by mistake and getting hurt by a car.

I also went for my first free-run in the park, but some nasty things called stinging nettles made my paws sore. Joe made them better with a dock leaf.

Joe hadn't got a photo of Patch at training or on the walk so he added one of Patch cuddled up to Squeaker on a cushion instead.

Sam's day had been a particularly tough one as the physiotherapists on the rehabilitation ward put him through his paces. Without the use of his legs he needed to increase his upper-body strength to compensate. He'd been strong before and had lifted weights, but now his legs were a dead weight and it was much harder to do pull-ups with them dragging him down.

Ten pull-ups weren't too hard; twenty were a bit of a struggle. But the physiotherapists wanted him to do fifty and his arm muscles were shaking by the end of the session.

After it was over he switched on his iPad and smiled as soon as he saw Patch's diary had been updated. He checked every day and the nurses and other patients already knew all about Patch – and Sam's hope that the puppy would become his Helper Dog one day soon.

Reading about Patch always made his day.

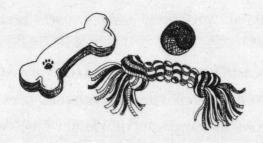

Chapter 13

Joe and Patch went to their first Helper Dogs class on Wednesday. This time Joe's mum came with them.

As soon as Patch saw Ollie, Lenny's retired Helper Dog, he bounded over to him.

'You'd think they already knew each other,' Joe's mum smiled as Patch stood up on his back paws to get closer to the much bigger Ollie, his little tail wagging like mad. Ollie's tail wagged too, but not as quickly as Patch's.

'Young pups can be a bit much for older dogs sometimes,' Lenny said. 'I don't take Ollie along to my pre-puppy classes because of it.'

Joe and his mum were the first to arrive, but soon other people came in with their dogs and puppies-in-training. The Helper Dogs were much better behaved than the pre-puppy class puppies had been, and they didn't go for a run outside before the class started.

Ollie went to greet each person and their dog with a tail wag, and Patch followed him like a little shadow so he got to greet everyone too.

'Oh, aren't you just gorgeous,' said a lady called Ann with a black Lab called Dora.

Joe watched as the volunteers put the dog mats and toys they'd brought with them next to the tethering rings spaced out along the sides of the walls.

'Helper Dogs have to get used to waiting quietly,' Lenny explained as the dogs lay down on their mats and were given a chew or a toy or usually both. 'Sometimes it's hard to learn, so we start early. We discourage barking because if a disabled person is taking his dog to work with him every day, he doesn't want the dog barking every time someone walks past his office. I don't think your teachers would like it much if Patch kept barking, either,' Lenny said to Joe.

Joe secretly thought it might make the lessons more interesting, though.

All of the other puppies in training were a lot older than Patch – most of them seemed to be five or six months old. And most of them were Labs and golden retrievers, but there was also one spaniel called Hamish.

Ann's black Labrador, Dora, was the oldest one there at seven months. 'She's leaving to go for her final assessment next week,' Ann told Joe's mum as they said hello. 'It's going to break my heart to see her go, but I know she'll be going to someone who needs her far more than I do.'

Joe didn't want to think about Patch leaving one day, so he took him to say hello to Hamish instead. The two dogs sniffed each other and wagged their tails. But when Patch tried to take Hamish's duck toy, Hamish reminded him with a soft growl that it wasn't his. Patch dropped the toy and Hamish wagged his tail to show there were no hard feelings.

Once the dogs were all settled and the handlers had got a drink and a biscuit, they pulled some chairs round in a rough circle and Lenny formally introduced Joe and his mum to them.

'This is Joe and Mary, and more importantly this is little Patch. Pass Patch to Olivia, Joe.'

Patch had been sitting on Joe's lap, but now he handed the puppy to Olivia, Hamish's handler, who was sitting on the other side of him, and she made a big fuss of Patch. A minute later she passed him on to the person sitting next to her.

'It's good for Patch to get used to being handled by different people besides you and your mum,' Lenny told Joe.

Patch seemed to think being stroked by different people was fine, but he was over the moon when he was finally returned to Joe.

'He's definitely Joe's dog,' Mum smiled.

'Be prepared for when he has to leave,' Ann warned Joe, but Joe was only half listening because Patch was licking at his ear. He couldn't imagine not having Patch with him. He wasn't even going to think about it.

Lenny put a small rug close to the wall next to Hamish for Joe to tether Patch to along with a toy and a puppy chew. But Patch didn't want to be tethered and he whined and tried to pull away from his lead to get back to Joe. Then he tried yapping to let Joe know he wanted to be back on his lap.

'Just ignore him when he's barking, and praise him and maybe give him the odd treat when he's quiet,' Lenny said.

'I always bring a chew and Dora's squeaky mouse toy when she has to be tethered,' Ann said. 'I hope wherever she goes next gives her chews and toys.'

'Olivia, how's your week with Hamish been?' Lenny asked her. 'Hamish is one of our more lively dogs,' Lenny said, winking at Joe and his mum.

Joe looked over at Hamish, who was gnawing on his chew. Patch saw him looking and yapped to make it clear that he didn't like being tethered. Joe looked away and Lenny nodded.

Each of the volunteers reported back to Lenny on what had happened with their puppy that week and what they had done together. The volunteers offered each other advice, but Joe and his mum just listened.

Patch whined again and stood up, looking thoroughly miserable. Joe started to feel miserable too. Poor little Patch stuck halfway across the room. He hadn't even touched the chew. Joe wanted to go to Patch and comfort him, but someone else went first.

Ollie trotted over to Patch and lay down on his mat. Patch lay down beside him and was soon fast asleep, cuddled up to the older dog.

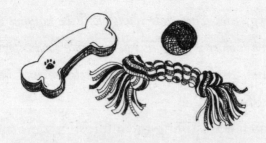

Chapter 14

Joe and Patch's second Helper Dogs class was also the last before the school term started. Joe's mum was supposed to take him and Patch in the car, but at the last minute she had to take a work call.

'I'm so sorry, Joe. We'll have to miss the class this week. I just don't have a choice.'

But Joe didn't want to miss it.

'I'll take Patch on the bus,' he said.

Mum looked doubtful. 'Are you sure?'

'Yes,' Joe said. 'It's only a few stops.' In the Helper Dogs manual he'd read that: *Everything a puppy tries when he's young, he'll be happier to do when he's older. As long as you make it a good experience for him. And that means being relaxed and happy yourself.*

Patch was sniffing the interesting new smells at the bus stop when Mr Humphreys came along. Patch immediately started wagging his tail and tried to jump up at their neighbour because he was so excited to see him. Joe wondered if Patch remembered him as the man with the water snake.

'What on earth are you two doing here? Car broken down?' he asked them.

'No – Mum's got a meeting so Patch and I are going to the Helper Dogs class on the bus,' Joe told him.

'Are you indeed? You can tell me more about Helper Dogs on the way,' Mr Humphreys remarked as the bus drew up.

Patch wasn't too sure about the noisy bus monster and he tried to run away as it shuddered to a halt. Joe didn't make a big thing of it and tried to keep calm.

'That's it, Patch, come on. What's this?' Joe said as he held out a treat for Patch's nose to aim for. The steps were wide for a little puppy, but Patch managed to jump up them, then take his treat and crunch it up as the other passengers watched him.

'How much is it for my puppy?' Joe asked.

'He's a Helper Dog in training,' Mr Humphreys said loudly from behind him.

'No charge for assistance dogs,' the driver said.

Mr Humphreys held out his bus pass and the driver waved him on. 'No charge for me, either.'

Fortunately the bus wasn't very busy. Patch lay down at Joe's feet and investigated the laces of Mr Humphreys' shoes. Joe wouldn't have said Patch was exactly happy to be on the juddery bus, but he put up with it for the few stops that they went.

'So what's this Helper Dogs thing all about then?' Mr Humphreys asked.

'It's a charity that provides highly trained dogs for disabled people,' Joe recited straight from the Helper Dogs manual. 'Lots of them go to soldiers like my dad . . . like my dad was. Once Patch is old enough and has finished his initial training, he'll go to a soldier called Sam. He was badly hurt trying to help some other soldiers.'

'I see,' Mr Humphreys nodded. 'A very important job for your little imp then.'

'Yes,' Joe agreed. It was a very important job indeed. 'My dad wanted us to train a dog like Patch and help a soldier who's been . . . been injured and needs him,' Joe said. But even as he said the words, he still couldn't quite believe that Patch might one day not be with him.

'Your dad would be pleased.'

'Yes. Yes, he would.'

'I used to have a dog, you know,' Mr Humphreys said.

'Did you?' said Joe. He'd thought Mr Humphreys hated dogs.

'Billy, his name was, lived for twenty years before I lost him. Smartest dog I've ever known,' Mr Humphreys said, and his eyes turned misty as he remembered. 'Well behaved too.'

'What sort of dog was he?' Joe asked.

'A bitzer,' Mr Humphreys said.

'I haven't heard of those,' Joe said. 'What do they look like?'

'Billy looked a bit like a Jack Russell and a bit like a Border collie with bits of goodness knows what else too. He was a *bits of this* and *bits of that* dog,' Mr Humphreys said, his false teeth grinning at his own joke. 'What you'd call one of those designer doodle dogs these days.'

The bus pulled in and it was time for Joe and Patch to get off. Mr Humphreys stayed on board as he was going into the town centre.

'See you soon,' he called after them.

Patch's tail wagged happily once they were safely on the ground and the noisy, smelly bus had driven away.

Mr Humphreys waved out of the window.

'No need to tether your dogs, it's a supermarket trip today,' Lenny said when they arrived.

'Supermarket?' Joe asked. He hadn't even had a chance to tell Lenny about going on the bus yet.

'Here, Joe, you'll need this for Patch.' Lenny threw Joe a tiny Helper Dogs-in-training jacket.

'Hold still,' Joe laughed as Patch put his head down instead of through the jacket neck. Then Patch saw Ollie, and Joe was only just in time to catch him and secure the Velcro jacket straps before Patch could run over to his friend.

Patch had barely had a chance to sniff Ollie before they were off again.

'Helper Pups need to go to all sorts of places,' Lenny explained. 'Definitely the supermarket, but also on buses . . .'

'We came on a bus,' Joe began to say, but Lenny was too busy talking to hear him.

'. . . and trains. Ollie and I will come on that trip with you and Patch, Joe. Ollie loves trains. Then there are schools, churches, hospitals, dentists, hairdressers and of course all sorts of shops.'

Patch trotted along beside Joe, looking over at his friend Ollie, who was with Lenny, every now and again.

'I phoned ahead and told them we were coming as there are quite a lot of us today,' Lenny said as they trooped towards the supermarket entrance.

Patch didn't like the automatic door, but Ollie went through, so the puppy followed the older dog in.

The customers and staff were very pleased to see them – especially Patch.

'Oh, isn't he lovely.'

'Is he new?'

'Is it all right if I say hello?'

All the pups had their Helper Dog-in-training jackets on and some of the more experienced volunteers pointed out that the coat also said PLEASE DO NOT DISTURB ME, I'M BEING TRAINED.

Joe didn't think he'd ever be able to stop anyone from saying hello to Patch because he knew how much he'd have wanted to say hello if he'd seen him. Patch wagged his tail happily whenever anyone came up to them. He was such a friendly little dog.

But all the new sights and smells, as well as all the attention on top of the bus trip, were exhausting for a young puppy. As the manager of the store came over to stroke him, Patch lay down in the middle of the aisle and fell fast asleep.

Joe wasn't sure what to do. None of the other Helper Dog volunteers were nearby and the manager had moved on.

'Wake up, Patch,' he said, gently tugging at his lead, but all Patch did was roll over.

'Oh, look at him. Isn't he sweet,' customers said as they wheeled their trolleys round him.

Patch didn't stir.

Joe was afraid someone might accidentally step on the puppy – and also that he might have an accident when he woke up. Patch still needed to 'go' almost as soon as he opened his eyes!

Joe couldn't see Lenny anywhere. If there'd been a trolley nearby he'd have put Patch in it, but there wasn't, so Joe lifted Patch up and carried him outside. He waited on the bench by the door with Patch asleep on his lap until Lenny found him.

'I wondered where you'd got to. Been looking all over the shop for you,' he said.

'Patch got tired and went to sleep on the floor.'

'I can see that.' Lenny laughed. 'A sleepy pup is perfect for taking on a train.'

'He's already been on a bus today,' Joe said.

'Excellent! It'd be good to take him on a train too before you go back to school,' Lenny said. 'You wouldn't want to miss his first train trip would you?'

Joe shook his head. He wanted to share every experience that he could with Patch.

'Let's do it this afternoon then,' Lenny said.

Back at the centre Patch and Ollie had a long drink of water followed by a chew stick. Joe had a Coke and a packet of crisps, and Lenny had a mug of tea and a biscuit.

'Ready, then?' Lenny asked, and Joe nodded.

Patch was much happier being in the back of Lenny's Helper Dogs van with Ollie there too. He gave his friend's ear a lick.

'We'll just go one stop and then back again,' Lenny said, pulling into the car park.

Joe stood well back from the platform, but even so Patch flinched when a fast train went speeding past.

'It's OK, Patch,' Joe said as he crouched down to stroke the trembling puppy. 'Nothing to be scared of.'

Patch still flinched a little as the next train sped past, but not as much as before, and he looked up at Joe as if to say, *That wasn't so bad, was it?* Ollie wasn't bothered about trains at all. He even wagged his tail as they zoomed along the rails.

'Before he retired Ollie was always going out and about on trains with his disabled partner,' Lenny said. 'Ollie's probably been on more train trips than you or I have combined.'

The next train was the right one, and Joe and Patch followed Lenny and Ollie on board. It wasn't busy as it was late morning and they sat at a table for the short journey. Patch copied Ollie and lay down next to him under the table.

'What lovely dogs,' one of the few other passengers commented. 'Are they father and son?'

'No,' Lenny told the passenger. 'Just friends.'

Joe suddenly found himself wishing more than anything that he could be on a train with his dad.

There was another chew and a game of ball for Patch and a snooze for Ollie in a nearby park before they headed back on the train. Then Lenny gave Joe and Patch a lift home in the van.

'Patch did really well today,' he told Joe as he dropped them off. 'He's going to make someone a fine Helper Dog one day.'

Patch slept all afternoon while Joe got ready for going back to school the next day. But he was wide awake and full of energy by the evening. So Joe took him for a walk round the block. It was later than they usually went and already dark.

As he walked, Joe thought about the return to school. He couldn't bear the thought of the other kids asking him questions about his dad. What would he say? He didn't want to talk about it to anyone. For once he wasn't paying much attention to Patch, who trotted along on a loose lead a little ahead of him, and Joe didn't notice when the puppy stepped off the kerb.

Suddenly a car came down the street, its headlights bright. Realizing just in time, Joe pulled Patch back and the puppy skittered behind Joe's legs.

'It's OK, you don't need to be scared,' Joe said, crouching down to stroke the little dog. He should have been paying more attention. It was just like Lenny had taught them with the gate exercise. *I should have been in front*, Joe told himself. *I should have been watching*.

Patch looked up at him, but he didn't wag his tail. He trembled with fear. The day had been a very long one with lots of new sights and sounds and smells. Almost too much for a young puppy to take in, and the car lights had really frightened him.

'I won't let anything hurt you,' Joe said softly.

And in his heart he knew he'd do anything to protect the little pup.

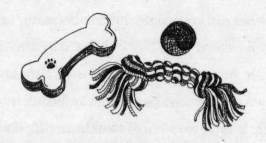

Chapter 15

Although he left for school in plenty of time to get there, Joe dawdled and went down one street twice so that when he arrived the bell had already rung. He ran in at the last minute, breathing a sigh of relief that no one had had a chance to speak to him.

The classroom was very noisy with everyone talking about their holidays as he went in.

'Hey, Joe,' Charlie said. 'Good to have you back.'

Joe took his seat as their teacher, Miss Addams, came in.

'What did you do during the holidays, miss?' Charlie asked her.

'Oh, just trekked through the Himalayas,' Miss Addams told her with a smile.

'Ooh, nice; we went to Benidorm. My dad got sunburnt and my brother pushed my wheelchair into the swimming pool,' Charlie said.

'We went on safari,' boasted Thomas.

'I went to my gran's,' said Ben.

'I just stayed at home,' said Sheila.

Joe hoped Miss Addams wouldn't ask him how he was. He didn't want to tell everyone about the funeral. But then he remembered Patch.

'I got a puppy,' he chipped in, and everyone stopped talking over each other and listened to him instead. 'His name's Patch.'

'Oh, cute,' said Ben.

'What sort is he?' asked Sheila.

'He's not just a pet puppy,' Joe said. 'He's training to be a Helper Dog when he grows up.'

At that moment the bell rang and it was time for the first assembly of term. Joe and the rest of his class sped down the corridor to the hall. All the children had to sit on the floor, apart from Charlie.

'We have a very special visitor with us today,' Mr Potter the head teacher said once everyone was there. 'I'll give you a clue. He's got four legs and he is very furry.'

'Is it a lion?' asked Charlie loudly and everyone laughed.

'No, not a lion,' Mr Potter replied, looking towards the side of the stage.

Suddenly, Joe's mum stepped out from behind the curtain, accompanied by Patch on his lead. His little tail wagged happily and there was a collective *Awww* from the assembled children. Joe could hardly believe it. Patch was really there, up on the stage in front of his whole school.

'He's so cute,' cooed Charlie.

'What's his name?' asked Thomas.

'How come he's at our school?' Daniel wanted to know.

'Why's he got one black ear and one yellow one?' asked Ben.

'Joe, perhaps you can come out here and answer some of these questions?' the head teacher said.

Joe could feel all of his classmates' eyes staring at him as he stood up and went to the front. Patch was so happy to see him that his little tail wagged a million times a minute, and he licked and licked Joe's face when Mum gave him the puppy to hold.

'Thank you,' Joe whispered.

'I thought he might be missing you,' his mum said with a wink.

'Now, little Patch is a very special puppy, isn't he, Joe?' the head teacher said.

'Yes, he's a Helper Pup,' Joe explained, 'and one day he's going to make a big difference to a disabled soldier's life.'

'Patch is still very young, though, isn't he?'

'He's twelve weeks old,' Joe said.

'Patch will be coming into school with Joe sometimes, but when he's here, he's working. Patch is going to be an assistance dog. He's not just a pet, so if you want to say hello to him you must ask Joe first, and only one at a time because I don't want you all trying to stroke him at once. Do any of you have any questions for Joe?'

Lots of children did. But the main thing everyone wanted to know was how they could become Helper Dog volunteers and bring a puppy to school too.

At the end of the assembly the head teacher made everyone wait so that Joe and Patch and then the rest of his class could go back to their classroom first.

'Even though I know you're just trying to be friendly, just think how scary it must be for a little pup to have a stampede of children wanting to say hello,' he told them. 'You're frightening enough for me and I'm much older than he is!'

Joe took Patch out to the playground before he headed back just in case the little dog had an accident in class.

'What a lovely puppy,' Miss Addams said when Joe and Patch reappeared. 'I'm so glad he's going to be visiting us.'

'So is he going to be for someone who's in a wheelchair like me?' Charlie asked. 'Could I have him one day?'

'No, he's going to help a wounded soldier,' Joe said. 'He's a man called Sam and –'

'Might not be in a wheelchair then,' interrupted Archie. 'My uncle got wounded, but he's got a prosthesis.'

'What's that?' asked Ben.

'When one of your limbs has been amputated and you're given a man-made part to replace it. My uncle's was made using a three-D printer.'

'But if the soldier that Patch goes to needs to be in a wheelchair,' Joe asked Charlie, 'is there anything you think might be really useful for Patch to learn to help him?'

'Hundreds of things,' Charlie said, rolling her eyes. 'But the most useful one is this.' She dropped a pencil on the floor. As Joe and the others stared down at it she said, 'You could all pick it up without a second's thought, but if I drop my pencil, or anything, I have to ask someone to please pick it up for me, and if there's no one to ask, it stays there or I stay there until someone comes along.'

'Right,' Joe said thoughtfully, and he sat down at his desk while Patch sat under it. Joe was pretty sure he could teach Patch to pick up a pencil and give it back to him, no problem, but he wasn't going to tell Charlie that until he'd tried it first.

Joe's mum came to pick Patch up after an hour and take him home. School wasn't so much fun after Patch had gone, but at least no one bothered to ask him anything about his dad. All they wanted to do was ask him about Patch.

Back at home, Patch missed Joe. Joe had always been with him all day, every day before.

When Patch needed to go outside, he barked at the back door and Joe's mum came downstairs and let him out.

'Why don't you come upstairs with me?' she said, and Patch followed her. He went to sleep under her desk, but as soon as Joe came in he raced back downstairs, barking his high puppy bark. He was so excited to have Joe back that he ran round and round in circles, then raced to grab Squeaker and ran back to Joe, his tail wagging like crazy.

'He's very pleased to see you,' Joe's mum laughed.

'Not as pleased as I am to see him,' said Joe, hugging Patch and letting him lick his face. 'I couldn't believe my eyes when he came to school.'

'I thought it might make your first day back a little easier,' Joe's mum admitted.

'It did.'

'Your school is fine about Patch coming in, by the way. Not every day, though, because it'll be too hard for anyone to get any work done with him there.'

Joe nodded. Any time was fine with him, although all the time would have been best.

'Come on, Patch,' he said, and the puppy ran after him for a game of ball in the garden.

After tea, Joe and Patch went up to his bedroom. He thought about Charlie and how tough some things were for her that were simple for him to do. Sitting on the chair, Joe dropped a pencil on the floor and tried to reach it without getting up or moving his legs. It wasn't easy. In fact it was just about impossible to do without falling off the chair. How did

Charlie manage every day, he wondered. Before now he'd never thought too much about it – she never seemed any different from anyone else in the class and she was much noisier and nosier than most!

Patch tilted his head to one side and watched Joe as he tried unsuccessfully to reach the pencil.

'Get it, Patch,' Joe told the puppy, pointing at the pencil. 'Get it.'

Patch went over to the pencil, put his nose to it and then looked back at Joe.

'That's it. Get it,' Joe said. 'Please.'

Patch carefully picked up the pencil in his mouth as Joe held his breath. The pencil was much thinner and harder to grasp than any of his toys and it fell out of the puppy's mouth.

'Get it, Patch.'

Patch carefully picked up the pencil again.

'Bring it here,' Joe instructed, tapping his lap,

and Patch slowly walked over to him with the pencil still in his mouth. Joe took it from him.

'Good dog! You're such a good dog,' Joe said, making a big fuss of Patch and giving him a treat from the bag he now kept on his bookshelf.

Patch wagged his tail and then went over and picked up another pencil Joe had forgotten about that had rolled under his desk. It felt a bit awkward in his mouth, but he managed to hold on and then dropped it in Joe's lap.

Joe laughed and laughed. 'You really are one amazing dog,' he said. 'One amazing dog.'

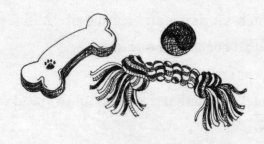

Chapter 16

When Joe was about to leave for school the next day, Patch raced to the front door as well.

'Sorry, Patch, you can't come,' Joe told him, although he really wished the puppy could.

Patch tried to push his way past him and out of the door. Joe couldn't really mean that he had to stay behind. Where Joe went, he went – that was the way it was and the way it should be.

Joe felt awful.

'No, Patch,' he said. He held out his hand, palm facing the puppy, in the 'stay' command.

Patch sat down and looked up at him with his head cocked on one side.

'Good puppy.'

Patch whined and was about to stand up.

'No.'

He sat down again as Joe opened the door and went out.

From behind the door, Joe heard Patch give a cry of protest that tore through him, but he made himself walk on down the path and along the road to school.

Patch lay by the front door with his head resting on his paws and that's where Joe's mum found him.

'Come on, Patch, how about some breakfast?' she said.

Patch trotted behind her as she headed to the kitchen, but his tail didn't wag like it usually did. He sat down and watched her as she poured food into his bowl and he ate it up because he was always hungry, but he wasn't a happy pup. As soon as he'd finished, he went back to the front door, whined and sat down on the mat to wait for Joe to come home.

'Where's Patch?' Charlie asked as soon as Joe got to school.

'He's not coming today,' he told her. 'But he's coming again next Monday.'

The rest of Joe's classmates were also disappointed that Patch wasn't with Joe.

'He was so cute.'

'And so good – my dog would have freaked out if I'd brought him into school.'

'I asked my mum if we could have a Helper Pup too, but she said she was allergic to dogs.'

'It's too much for a little pup to come to school every day,' Miss Addams told them. 'Much as we'd all like him to. Now, do you want to hear about this year's school day trip or not?'

Every term their year got to have a day out.

'This time we're going to . . . Fridlington-on-Sea.'

'Miss, miss,' Charlie said, 'can Joe bring Patch along?'

'Ooh yes. That'd be good!' various other children in the class enthused.

'Please can he, miss?' Charlie asked. 'You'd like him to, wouldn't you, Joe?'

Joe nodded. There was nothing he'd like more than to bring the puppy along. He was sure he'd have an amazing time and Lenny was always saying Helper Pups needed lots of learning experiences. Plus Patch would get to see the sea!

'I don't see why not,' Miss Addams said. 'I'll have to check to make sure, of course. But would you like to bring him with us, Joe – if he's allowed?'

'Yes, I would. But I'll have to check with Helper Dogs first,' he said.

*

The day seemed to take forever to be over. Joe ran all the way home to see Patch. He'd missed him so much.

Patch stood up, his tail wagging, as Joe ran gasping up the path and put his key in the lock. Patch had spent nearly all day waiting for him and at last Joe was home.

The puppy twirled round and round in a circle of excitement and licked and licked Joe's face to show how happy he was while Joe got his breath back. Then Joe phoned Lenny to check if it was OK to take Patch on the school trip.

'The more Patch gets to experience, the better,' Lenny said, just as Joe had hoped he would.

'You're going to see the sea, Patch!' he told the puppy. 'You'll love it, plus there's lots of sand to dig in too.'

Patch wagged his tail and then dropped his ball at Joe's feet as a hint that now he was home it was time for a game.

'OK then,' Joe said, and the two of them headed out to the garden with Patch leading the way.

The next day, and the one after that, Patch waited all day at the door for Joe to come home.

'He knows, you know,' Joe's mum said when he came home from school on Thursday.

'Knows what?'

'Knows when you're coming home. He waits by the door and sits up suddenly when you get close. Long before you've put your key in the lock. I don't know how he knows, but he just does. I'd have said he could tell the time, but dogs can't do that, can they?'

Joe hugged Patch to him. 'I wish I could take him to school with me every day,' he said. 'It's a million times better when he's there too.'

*

On Friday, when Joe got home from school Patch wasn't waiting at the front door for him. Joe couldn't help feeling a little disappointed.

'Patch! Patch, where are you?' he called.

He could hear Mum upstairs on the phone, but Patch wasn't with her when he went to look. Joe gazed out of the office window.

There was Patch in the back garden, looking up at the wooden fence on the opposite side to Mr Humphreys' high hedge. Something was sitting on top of the fence. Something very interesting that Patch had never seen before. He kept dead still and looked at it, and the interesting thing kept dead still and looked back at him.

When Joe came out through the kitchen door Patch's tail flipped back and forth in greeting, but he didn't move from his spot.

Joe looked at the cat on top of the fence. It was a large black and white one, about the same size as Patch. He'd never seen it in their garden before.

'Here, puss,' Joe called to the cat. He thought it would be a good idea if Patch could make friends with it. 'Here, puss.'

But the cat stayed where it was on top of the fence, just looking at Patch. The little dog whined as if to say he wished the cat would come down and say hello.

Joe ran into the house and grabbed a can of tuna from the cupboard and pulled the ring-pull to open it. Then he ran back out with a saucer, but stopped when he reached the back door and walked slowly into the garden so as not to frighten the cat.

'Here, puss,' Joe called as he emptied the tuna out on to the saucer. Patch thought the tuna smelt very fine indeed and came to investigate.

'Leave it,' Joe said and Patch sat back on his puppy bottom and looked at Joe, begging for the lovely-smelling tuna with his eyes.

The cat looked down at the food and its tail swished to and fro. Joe was sure the cat must want the fish, but it didn't come down for it even though Joe waited for what felt like ages. Finally he tipped half of the tuna on to the path for the cat.

'You'll get rats, dropping food on the ground like that, and rats aren't discriminating about whose garden they go into. So if you get rats, I'll get rats,' Mr Humphreys' voice said from the top of the stepladder he was standing on to trim his hedge. 'And then you'll really need that cat. I wouldn't let a cat in my garden. My Billy would have seen it off. That cat was over here this afternoon and I squirted it with my hosepipe – didn't like that, I can tell you.'

Mr Humphreys hadn't much liked getting wet with the hosepipe either when Patch had visited his garden, Joe thought.

'Here, Patch, you can have the rest,' Joe said, and Patch happily ran after him as he went back inside.

As soon as Joe put the saucer down, Patch's head went down too. He licked up the tuna and then he licked his lips as if to say the fish was just as delicious as he'd hoped it would be.

Joe watched through the kitchen window as the cat jumped down from the fence and went to investigate the tuna now that they'd gone. He only let Patch outside when the cat had finished.

Patch scampered over to say hello, but the cat jumped back up on to the fence and scooted along it to the garages at the back of the houses. Patch sat down and stared up at the spot where the cat had been and whined.

When they went back inside, Joe wrote Patch's online diary.

Today something sat on my fence and stared at me. I wagged my tail, but it didn't come down. It liked fish, though – just like I do.

Sam laughed as he read the diary entry. He was glad Patch had made a new friend. He'd made lots of friends himself at the rehabilitation hospital and he was going to miss them when he left, but he couldn't wait to start his new life with Patch.

Joe made himself a sandwich for dinner and one for his mum too and took it up to her in her office.

'This is very nice,' she said, taking a bite of the tuna and tomato sandwich. Patch stared at her plate meaningfully.

'Come on, Patch,' Joe said, and they headed back downstairs.

On the Helper Dogs website he'd seen a photograph of a dog getting the laundry out of the washing machine and he wanted to try and teach Patch to do it too.

Joe put Squeaker on the rim of their front-loading washing-machine drum.

'Get it, Patch, get Squeaker,' Joe said, pointing at the toy on the edge of the washing machine. 'Get it.'

Patch trotted over, picked up Squeaker and brought the toy snake back to Joe, ready for a game.

They played with Squeaker for a few minutes and then Joe put the toy back, only this time he put it slightly further inside the drum.

'Get it, Patch, get Squeaker.'

Patch's tail wagged as he went to retrieve his toy. He liked this new game.

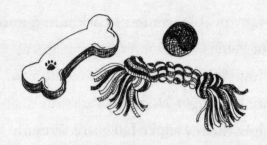

Chapter 17

On Monday, as soon as Joe and Patch walked into the playground, everyone crowded around them, wanting to say hello.

'He's grown since you brought him in before,' stated Ben.

'They should let him come to school every day,' said Daniel.

'Don't crowd him too much,' Joe warned, and the children pushed each other back to make a path for him and Patch to walk through. But it took ages for them to get to class because so many people wanted to ask him questions about Patch.

'How long is he going to live with you?'

'Are all Helper Dogs Labradors?'

'How many Helper Dogs are there?'

When he got to class, Joe went over to Charlie's desk and, without saying anything, knocked her pencil to the floor.

'What did you do that for?' she said indignantly.

'Get it, Patch,' Joe said softly as he pointed at the pencil.

Patch carefully picked up the pencil and gave it to Joe, who put it back on Charlie's desk. Charlie stared at the pencil for a long time and then she said, 'When it was my birthday, my cards dropped through the letterbox on to the carpet and I couldn't even pick them up.'

'Patch could have done that for you,' Joe said. 'Although they'd probably have been a bit soggy from his dribble.'

'I wouldn't have minded a bit,' she grinned. 'You're one fantastic pup, Patch.'

Patch stood on his back legs and rested his front paws on the arm of her wheelchair so she could stroke him.

'One fantastic pup,' she said as she buried her face in his fur.

Patch was having far too much fun with the children to want to go home when Joe's mum came to pick him up.

'Can't he stay a bit longer?' pleaded Charlie, who'd now got Patch on her lap in the wheelchair.

'He's been so good, Mum,' Joe said.

Mum shook her head. 'Sorry, love, but Lenny told us Patch should only stay for a morning or afternoon at first. As he gets older he can come to school for longer,' she told Charlie.

Patch hopped off Charlie's lap so Joe's mum could give him a stroke. He'd been petted by just about everyone he'd met all morning and had also had his first taste of crunchy crisps.

'I wish he could be here all day, every day,' Charlie sighed. And Joe wished that too.

'Once he's a little older,' Joe's mum said as she headed out of the door.

Patch looked back at Joe and the other children as he trotted along beside her. He wasn't ready to go home yet either. He gave a whine as they left the school and walked towards the car.

'In you get, Patch. Joe will be home before you know it,' Joe's mum reassured the pup as she opened the hatchback boot. Patch put his front paws on the boot edge and then hopped up and into his crate.

'Good boy.'

Patch didn't like his crate, but he liked Squeaker, and Joe's mum had put the snake toy inside it.

Patch gave Squeaker a *hello* gnaw on the ear and then held him in his paws on the short journey home. The puppy's eyelids felt heavy and he closed them.

'Here we are,' Joe's mum said, opening the boot and waking Patch up.

Patch blinked.

'Oh, you do look sleepy,' Mum smiled. 'Come on, how about some food and then you can have a nice long nap.'

Even though he was very tired, Patch managed to gobble up all of his puppy-food lunch and have a big drink of water before he went out into the garden.

Joe's mum came out into the garden with a sandwich and a cup of tea. But she'd only taken one bite when her work phone rang upstairs and she had to run back to her bedroom office.

Patch had never been left alone in the garden before. He sniffed at the leaf-sweeping brush and tried a bit of bird food that had fallen off the bird table.

Next to the bird table there was a shady bush and Patch lay down under it. Almost as soon as his eyes had closed he was fast asleep. Even the metallic sound of Mr Humphreys clipping his hedge in the garden next door didn't disturb him.

But the shouting did.

'Get out of it. Go on – scat, cat!'

Patch opened his eyes and raised his head a little off the ground, but he didn't get properly up. He could see a pair of shears waving wildly above the top of next-door's hedge, but suddenly there was an almighty crash, and a black and white cat came running into Patch's garden.

Patch sprang to his feet and wagged his tail, but the cat didn't want to play and jumped up on to the back wall and scuttled away.

There was more shouting from next door. Patch sniffed at the spot behind next-door's hedge where the voice was coming from and started to burrow and scrape at the bottom of the fence.

When Joe came home from school later, he was surprised to find that, once more, Patch wasn't waiting for him. He was usually at the front door, but not today.

'Patch,' he called. 'Patch, where are you?'

But the puppy didn't come running to him.

'Mum, have you got Patch with you?' he called up the stairs.

'He's in the garden,' she called back.

But when Joe went out into the garden Patch wasn't there either. His stomach churned with worry. He couldn't have wandered off, could he? Could Patch have somehow got out? He didn't know what he'd do if –

He didn't let himself think about the possibilities. He had to find the little pup!

Joe ran back inside and upstairs to his bedroom, but Patch wasn't in there, nor was he in the bathroom.

'Patch has gone!' he shouted to his mum as he ran back downstairs again. He checked in the front garden and the lounge, and then went out into the back garden again, getting more and more desperate all the time.

'Patch, Patch, where are you?' he yelled as loudly as he could.

'Over here,' Mr Humphreys called from behind the hedge. 'Your puppy's over here with me.'

Joe scrambled over the fence at the end of the garden, hoping Patch hadn't caused too much trouble. But he couldn't believe his eyes when he found Mr Humphreys lying flat on his back on the grass with Patch lying beside him. Patch jumped up and ran over to Joe.

'What's happened? Are you OK? I'm so sorry . . .' Joe said as Mr Humphreys let out a loud groan of pain. 'I won't let Patch in your garden again. I'll board up wherever he got in and maybe put some plants in front of it to stop him –'

'It wasn't Patch's fault,' Mr Humphreys said. 'If it wasn't for him, I'd be in a much sorrier state than I'm in now. I think my leg or at least my ankle's broken. Blasted cat.'

Then Joe noticed the stepladder that had toppled over on the ground.

'Joe?' Mum called from their back garden. 'Joe, are you OK? Did you find Patch?'

'He's here,' Joe called. 'But Mr Humphreys is injured.'

'Better call an ambulance,' Mr Humphreys said as Patch lay back down again beside him to comfort the old man.

Mr Humphreys stroked Patch's soft fur as they all waited for the ambulance to arrive. 'He's a good pup,' the old man said to Joe. 'He knew I was in trouble and came to help me.

Been stuck out here all afternoon waiting for you to come home, and he didn't leave my side once. He's a good dog, he is, and he's welcome in my garden any time. My Billy would have liked him.'

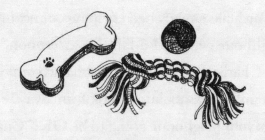

Chapter 18

Mr Humphreys had been gone in the ambulance
for an hour when the doorbell rang.

Joe opened it and was surprised to find
Charlie there. Patch was very excited to see her
and put his paws up on her lap so she could
stroke his head.

'Hello,' Joe said. He wondered what Charlie
was doing here.

'I thought of some more useful things Patch
could do,' Charlie said. 'You know, to help Sam
when he goes to live with him.'

'Patch has already been helping our next-door neighbour who had a fall this afternoon,' Joe told Charlie. 'He stayed with him and comforted him until an ambulance took him away.'

'Is your neighbour going to be OK?' Charlie asked. 'I always worry about falling out of my wheelchair.'

'He fell off his stepladder when he was trimming the back hedge,' Joe said. 'He's always up there trimming it.'

'Hello,' Mum said, appearing at the door behind Joe.

'You met Charlie at my school,' Joe said, and Mum nodded, then went to answer the phone, which was ringing.

'Do you want to come in?' Joe asked, but Charlie shook her head.

'I've got to get home, but I just wanted to tell you some of my ideas,' she said as she stroked Patch. 'You could teach him to find a mobile phone when it rings.'

'That's a good idea,' Joe replied, remembering how Ollie had done that at the training centre.

'And the TV remote. And I'd like a dog who could help me pull off my socks and put on my shoes.'

Joe nodded.

Charlie bit her bottom lip and then asked the question she'd been wanting to know the answer to ever since she'd met Patch.

'Do you think I could have a Helper Dog too?'

'Maybe,' Joe said. 'Why don't you ask Lenny at Helper Dogs? You could come along to one of the classes with me and Patch, if you like.'

'Yes, please,' Charlie said enthusiastically. 'Where did you get Patch from? Was it far away?'

'No, he came from Mrs Hodges. She only lives one street over,' Joe replied.

'I wonder if she's going to have any more Helper Pups?' Charlie pondered wistfully.

Joe didn't know the answer to that, but he thought if he were Charlie he'd want a Helper Pup too. 'She might be.'

Joe's mum came back to the door. 'That was the hospital. They said that Mr Humphreys will need to stay in for a few days. It was a nasty fall, especially for a man of his age, but thank goodness nothing was broken.'

'Good,' said Joe and Charlie at the same time.

'Are you coming in, Charlie?' Mum asked her, but Charlie shook her head.

'Swimming practice tonight. See you at school tomorrow, Joe.'

She pressed the button on her chair and whizzed off down the street.

'Come on, Patch. There're lots more things for you to learn,' Joe said. He knew he didn't need to teach Patch any of the things Charlie suggested, but Patch so loved learning new things that he thought he'd give it a try. And Charlie did have some good ideas.

Joe sat on one of the dining-room chairs and half pulled off one of his socks like he'd seen Lenny do at the Helper Dogs class so that it was flopping about at the end of his foot. Patch ran over to see what it was.

'Tug, tug, Patch,' Joe said, pointing to the toe of the sock. 'Tug, tug,' and he pulled at the sock himself. When it came off by mistake he gave a big cheer as if that was what he wanted to do, while Patch watched him, tail wagging, head on one side, as he worked out how to play this new game.

Joe half pulled the sock back on and waggled the end of it and then stretched it out. 'Tug, tug, Patch.'

Patch took hold of the end of the sock and Joe gave a cheer and made a big fuss of Patch when he managed to pull it off.

Patch picked up the sock and gave it to Joe to put back on so they could play again.

'Tug, tug, Patch.'

Patch tugged and Joe cheered and laughed when the sock came off.

'Good dog, Patch! Look, Mum! Look what Patch can do now,' he said when she came down from her office.

Patch's tail swayed at the sight of the sock waggling and Joe laughed as it came off once again. Working and playing with Patch made him so happy.

By bedtime, Joe's sock was looking a bit raggedy, but he didn't care. He patted the bed and Patch jumped up on to it and lay down beside him. Patch could now take off socks!

When Joe came home from school the next day, his mum led him to the kitchen and pointed out of the window. Patch and the black and white cat were lying together on the lawn. 'The cat's been here all day,' she smiled.

'That cat made Mr Humphreys fall off his stepladder, according to Mr Humphreys,' Joe said.

'Thank goodness he wasn't too badly injured,' Mum said. 'I really don't think he should be climbing up stepladders at his age. Not that Mr Humphreys would listen to anyone telling him that!'

Joe was glad Patch had another friend. He went to say hello. Patch came racing towards him as soon as he opened the kitchen door, but the cat jumped on to the fence and scampered away.

Mr Humphreys came home from hospital a week later and he brought with him some puppy treats for Patch.

'Don't let him eat them all up at once,' he said as he stroked the little dog. 'Don't want him getting sick. He's one fine pup, he is. One fine pup.'

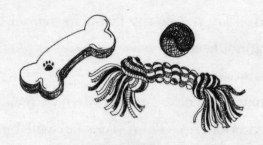

Chapter 19

As the summer turned to autumn, Patch gradually progressed from spending a morning at school with Joe to a whole day each week in the term leading up to Christmas. Joe thought the other children would take less notice of Patch after a while, but he was wrong. There were so many children at the school and only one Patch, so he was always treated like the star he was.

Charlie especially loved it when Patch came to school, which was usually on a Monday.

'Monday is now my favourite school day,' she announced.

'Mine too,' agreed Joe.

'Apart from next Tuesday when we're having our school trip. Then Tuesday will be my favourite day because that'll also be *Patch Day*,' Charlie grinned.

Joe had taught Patch to help Charlie get her jacket off by pulling gently at the sleeve, and he was always more than ready to pick up her pencil, or anything else she dropped.

'Thank you, Patch,' she said.

'Patch is going to pick up a pencil or pull off my socks at the Helper Dogs Open Day in two weeks' time,' Joe said. 'Lots of Helper Dogs will be there.'

'I'd really like to see all the things they can do,' Charlie told him as the bell rang and Miss Addams came in with the register. 'It would be the best thing ever if I could have my own Helper Dog one day.'

'You could come along this week, if you like,' Joe suggested. 'I bet Lenny wouldn't mind. Provided you didn't put the dogs off their work.'

'Really?' Charlie said, her eyes shining. 'I'd soooo like to.'

'I'll check and let you know,' Joe told her.

'Text me,' Charlie said, and Joe nodded.

'Quieten down now, everyone,' Miss Addams said. 'I need to take the register and then I want to go over the arrangements for our day trip to Fridlington. It's probably not going to be all that warm for a beach trip so make sure you wrap up well.'

'Miss,' Charlie said when Miss Addams had called out everyone's names.

'Yes, Charlie?'

'I bet Patch could take that register back to the office in his mouth.'

Charlie was always thinking of things for Patch to do, but sometimes she forgot to ask

Joe first. He tried not to mind, but it could be a bit annoying.

Miss Addams looked down at the register and then over at Joe.

'I suppose we could give it a try,' she said. 'If it's OK with you, Joe?'

Joe nodded and took the register from Miss Addams.

'Hold it, Patch,' he said, holding the register in front of Patch, who had never carried anything quite so large before.

Patch carefully took the register in his mouth and kept hold of it as Joe led the way along the corridor to the school office.

'Thank you very much,' said Mrs Hunt, the school secretary. 'Do you think Patch would like a small dog treat? I've got some in my handbag for my own dog, Suki. She's a poodle.'

Patch wagged his tail at the sight of the bag of treats.

'Oh, does he like these?' Mrs Hunt asked.

'I don't know,' Joe said. 'He's never had those ones before, but so far he's liked all the dog treats he's tasted.'

Patch gently took the first small bone-shaped treat Mrs Hunt offered him, and then the second and the third.

Lenny had told them not to over-treat the dogs at their last Helper Dogs class.

'Save some for Suki,' laughed Joe.

When Joe asked if he could bring Charlie along to the Saturday morning class with him, Lenny said that would be fine.

Patch loved going to the classes, but Charlie was even more excited than him.

'I've been waiting here for half an hour,' she said when they arrived. 'I didn't want to be late!' The November wind was freezing and Charlie shivered. 'Hope it's warmer inside.'

As soon as they went into the centre Patch raced round in circles. He was very excited to see his friend Ollie and even more excited when the other Helper Dogs-in-training arrived too and they could all play together freely instead of being tethered as they usually were.

Patch and the spaniel Hamish had a game of chase back and forth across the room.

'It's like a dog party,' Charlie grinned as she watched Patch and the other dogs sniff, wag tails and play together.

'What's going on?' Joe asked Lenny.

'Next Saturday, as you know, we're going to have our annual Helper Dogs Open Day to show people all of the hard work you've been doing over the past months, and the amazing things these chaps are capable of. So once everyone has arrived, we're going to practise for it today.'

'Come on,' Joe said to Charlie. 'I'll introduce you to some of Patch's friends.'

Just at that moment Joe noticed Ann come in with her dog Dora.

'I don't understand,' he said in surprise. 'What's Dora doing here? I thought she'd gone to become a Helper Dog.'

'She didn't pass her final assessment and so she came back to me,' Ann told him.

'Do dogs that fail the assessment always end up staying with their puppy parents?' Charlie asked, looking at Joe. 'Or do they go to other people who'd like them?'

Joe's heart was racing.

'Usually the puppy parent,' Ann replied. 'The dogs know us and we love them. But the Helper Dogs charity can't pay for anything any more if they fail. Lenny said Dora could still be part of the open day demonstration, even though she isn't going to be living with a disabled person. I've decided Dora and I are going to start visiting schools, and old people's homes and clubs, and anywhere else where they want to hear about the work that Helper Dogs do.'

'That sounds great,' said Charlie, 'doesn't it, Joe?'

But Joe wasn't listening any more. He was looking down at Patch. He thought about the soldier Sam who Lenny had talked about, who was hoping to have Patch come and live with him. Even though he was sure Sam would love him, he couldn't help really, *really* wanting Patch to stay with him forever and be his pet. But then he immediately felt bad for thinking that. He looked up and noticed Charlie watching him.

'Come on,' Joe said quickly, 'it looks like Lenny is ready to begin.' And they gathered round Lenny.

'Next Saturday I want each of the dogs to demonstrate individually one of the helpful jobs that Helper Dogs do. So what can your dogs do well?' he asked them all.

'Hamish likes to carry the newspaper home from the shop. He's always very careful and there's barely a mark or any dribble on it,' Olivia said, as she stroked the spaniel who would be going for his final assessment soon.

'Cody likes to pull the light cord. Stands up on his back legs to do it. Only problem is sometimes, if he wakes up in the middle of the night, he switches it on and then he wakes all of us up too,' laughed Ted.

'You can't take your shoes off in our house without Minnie wanting to take your socks off as well,' grinned David as Minnie nuzzled her head into his hand.

'Dora's very good at taking the washing out of the machine,' said Ann. 'Always has been, haven't you, Dora?'

Dora looked at Ann and wagged her tail at the sound of her name.

Joe told Lenny about Patch picking up small items that got dropped on the floor.

'He's really good at it!' chipped in Charlie.

Once everyone had their individual jobs to do at the open day they practised coming in and circling the room with their dogs.

'All the dogs should be on a nice loose lead, of course. Come in as I call out your dog's name. I'll also say who you are and how old your dog is,' Lenny explained.

'But not how old we are,' quipped Ann and everyone laughed.

Lenny rolled his eyes and continued. 'Then you circle slowly round the room so everyone can have a good look at your dog, and then you join your place at the end of the queue.'

'I feel really self-conscious walking round by myself,' Joan said.

'You're not by yourself,' Lenny told her. 'And believe me, no one's going to be looking at you. They'll all be too busy staring at Busby!'

Once they'd practised circling the room they went over their individual sequences.

'And that'll be it really,' Lenny said. 'I'll tell

everyone about the dogs and say how we're always looking for more volunteers. A piece about the event is going in the local press this week. Oh, and there should be a few people here who actually have fully trained Helper Dogs. I'm hoping they will say a few words about the difference having the dog living with them has made.

'Well done, everyone. I'll see you next Saturday for the big day. If any of you want to come early, I could do with some help putting up the Christmas tree and decorations. Might as well make the place look festive. And if any of you can make cakes or dog biscuits that'd be good too. Can never have too many cakes or dog biscuits for everyone afterwards.'

'I'm really looking forward to the open day,' said Charlie as they headed for home.

Joe was looking forward to it too, but he couldn't help thinking how lucky Ann was to have Dora back.

When he got in, Joe wrote about the rehearsal practice in Patch's diary.

As Sam read the entry, he hoped Patch would be coming to live with him soon. He felt like he knew the puppy already through the diary and couldn't wait to meet him.

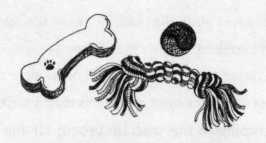

Chapter 20

The next Tuesday, the day of the field trip, it turned very cold. Joe filled his own backpack and then one for Patch for their day in Fridlington-on-Sea.

'Enough food and treats to last all day, plus three balls in case one gets lost, and we'd better have another as backup.' Patch loved playing ball. 'Squeaker too, of course,' he told Patch as the puppy watched him pack.

'One water bowl, one food bowl and your Helper Pup training vest too, naturally. Plus we'll need your dog blanket now it's started to get colder.'

The steps on to the school coach were even steeper than the ones on the bus they'd travelled on, but Patch managed to hop up them. The bus driver carried Charlie up the steps and put her in the front seat.

'Sit with me,' Charlie said as soon as Joe and Patch got on the bus. Everyone else wanted the popular pair to sit with them too, but Charlie had asked first so Joe sat with her. Patch lay down on the floor in between them for some of the time, and in the aisle down the centre of the coach so other children could stroke him for the rest.

'I'm really glad Patch got to come with us,' said Callum, who was sitting behind them.

'Me too,' agreed Daniel, his twin.

Two hours later they arrived and Patch hurried down the steps after Joe. The children and puppy headed out to explore the area with Miss Addams.

Fridlington-on-Sea had a sandy beach that stretched as far as you could see, whether you looked to the left or the right.

'Look, Patch, it's the sea!' Joe said, pointing to the wavy water ahead of them. He unclipped Patch's lead.

At first Patch didn't look too sure about the moving waves. But the children in Joe's class weren't scared of them. They raced towards the sea, pulling off their shoes and socks – all except Charlie. The sand was too soft for her chair to move on.

'Don't want to get stuck,' she said.

Patch looked up at her.

'But you go, Patch,' Charlie said. 'Go on. You can't come to the seaside and not have a paddle.'

Joe took his trainers and socks off and rolled up his jeans.

'Come on, Patch,' he said as they headed to the water.

Patch hopped back as the shallow waves came towards him, while the children ran into them and back before they got too wet.

'Nothing to be scared of,' Joe said as he waded out into the sea. 'Look.'

Once Patch saw that Joe wasn't afraid, he wasn't afraid either. He wagged his tail as he put first one paw and then the other into the sea. Soon Patch had pushed his way through the waves, and once the water got too deep, he started swimming.

Joe was terrified. What if Patch went too far? What if he got disorientated and kept swimming further away instead of back to him on the shore? What if he got too tired to keep on swimming?'

'Patch!' Joe called, trying to keep the desperation out of his voice. 'Patch! Come back.' But Joe had nothing to worry about as Patch doggy-paddled back towards the shore. Joe was so relieved when he came out of the water that he threw his arms round him and didn't care a bit about getting soaked as the puppy shook himself dry.

But, the next moment, Patch put his head down and started lapping thirstily at the salty water.

'No! No, don't drink the salty water, it'll make you feel sick,' Joe warned Patch, but it was too late. Patch coughed up a puddle of salty water. It hadn't tasted nice at all. He tried another lap in case it got any better, but it didn't.

'No, Patch. Leave it.'

All of a sudden a crab scuttled past. Patch tried to catch it with his paw, but the crab was too wily for him. It disappeared safely into the sand. Patch spotted another crab and tried to jump on that one instead, but with no luck. The little dog whined and dug at the sand where the crab had vanished.

Then Patch spotted a flock of seagulls further along on the sand and raced towards them. The squawking birds scattered in all directions.

'Hey, Patch!' Joe called. He threw a ball along the beach in the other direction and Patch turned and ran along the sand after it. The puppy's paws delighted in the feel of the unfamiliar sand and the wind ruffling through his fur.

Some of the children started making sandcastles. Others collected shells and pebbles to spell out their names on the beach.

'We'll do one for Patch too,' they said.

When Patch saw the children digging, he had to dig too. He dug and dug. Then he lay on his back with his legs in the air in the hole he'd made while the children laughed and Joe took photos of him.

'He's so funny.'

'This trip is so much better with Patch here too.'

Joe couldn't agree more.

After a sandwich on the beach for Joe and his classmates, and puppy food and a little bit of Joe's sandwich for Patch, they went to an open farm. As Patch was a Helper Dog in training, he was allowed to come in too.

'Just make sure you keep him on his lead at all times,' the farm manager told Joe.

'I will,' Joe promised.

'They've got decorations up,' Charlie smiled. 'I love the fairy lights. I can't wait for Christmas.'

Joe thought about Christmas. How had it come round so quickly? Last Christmas he, Mum and Dad had spent a whole day hanging their Christmas decorations together. He and Dad had saved the tree until last to do together. Joe sighed. Last Christmas felt like a lifetime ago.

'You OK?' Charlie asked him, looking concerned. Patch had his head tilted on one side and was looking up at Joe too.

'Course I am,' Joe said. 'Come on, let's go and meet some animals.'

Patch was very interested in all the different, exciting farm smells. So much so that for the first few minutes his nose was mostly down to the ground and sniffing.

But he looked up in shock when he heard a loud moo.

'It's a cow, Patch,' Joe told him. But Patch didn't look very sure about meeting one and he hid behind Joe's legs.

The cow, however, was very pleased to meet Patch and she put her head over the fence to look at him.

When the donkey saw Patch it started braying and Patch barked back. Joe looked from one of them to the other. It was as if they were having a proper conversation that only the two of them could understand.

'Come and see the piglets,' Charlie called when Patch and the donkey had stopped braying and barking.

There were five spotted piglets and they raced round their pen in a game of chase.

Patch wagged his tail and looked as if he'd very much like to join in the game.

Then a group of the children were given some corn to feed to the piglets, and when a piece dropped to the ground from Charlie's hand Patch licked it up and then spat it out again.

Finally they all clambered back on to the school bus to head home, and within moments of setting off, Patch had fallen asleep next to Joe.

As Joe looked out of the coach window he realized Christmas lights and decorations were starting to go up everywhere. He didn't feel Christmassy at all.

'Patch is snoring,' Charlie giggled, interrupting Joe's thoughts. Joe looked down at Patch. Well, this would be the puppy's first Christmas. That was something. Maybe it wouldn't be so bad after all.

When he got home Joe updated Patch's online diary.

First taste of seawater (bad), chase of seagulls (good) and digging in the sand (very good) today. But why are crabs so quick and cows so huge? And why wasn't I allowed to play with the piglets at the open farm? ☺

Joe added a smiley face after the entry because he knew by Patch's wagging tail and body language all day that the puppy had had a very good time. He was so pleased that Patch had been allowed to come on the trip too. Everything was so much better with him there.

When Sam read the diary he smiled. He'd make sure Patch got to see the sea again once he came to live with him. Maybe they could even go swimming in it together one day.

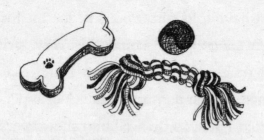

Chapter 21

On Saturday morning Joe was up early, ready for the open day. When he arrived at the Helper Dogs training centre, he found that Lenny had decorated the whole place for Christmas.

'I put them up after the class last night,' Lenny said.

Ollie looked hopefully at the little dog-treat bones tied to the tree with ribbons.

'Not yet,' Lenny told him with a smile.

Joe noticed Mr Humphreys arrive at the centre and take a seat at the front. Joe's mum must have told him about it. Joe bit his lip. Their neighbour could be very critical sometimes. What if he and Patch made a mistake in their demonstration? Joe desperately wanted Patch to do well and show everyone how hard they'd been working over the past months and how far the puppy had come.

'That puppy over there came to my rescue when I had a fall,' Mr Humphreys said in a very loud voice to the man sitting next to him. 'Amazing to think he's not yet six months old.'

Perhaps it would be OK after all, thought Joe.

Then Charlie arrived with her mum and dad and brother. She put her thumbs up and mouthed, 'Good luck,' to Joe. He grinned back, but he was still feeling quite nervous about appearing in public.

Mrs Hodges and Marnie turned up just before the demonstration started and Mrs Hodges waved at Joe.

'I don't know if I can do it,' Joe whispered to his mum, who was pouring water into the tea urn.

'Of course you can,' she said. 'You owe it to Patch to show everyone what a good puppy he is and how hard he's worked.'

When Mum put it like that, standing out in front of everyone didn't seem quite so bad. No one was there to look at Joe himself and he did want people to see what a great puppy Patch was.

'Joe, look,' his mum said and she nodded at the entrance. Joe glanced up and saw two soldiers coming in. One of them had lots of badges on his front and looked very senior. Perhaps he was a colonel, Joe thought. He remembered his dad explaining all the different ranks in the army to him when he was younger. The other soldier was in a wheelchair and had a large cream-coloured dog with him that looked like a cross between a Labrador and a poodle. *A labradoodle*, Joe thought to himself and smiled. The animal was clearly a Helper Dog.

Joe swallowed hard. This was what Patch had been training for. A soldier who needed him. A soldier like Sam.

The soldier stroked his Helper Dog and talked to him as they came in and took their places. Joe wondered if Dad might have known either of these soldiers. Maybe they were the reason his dad had known about Helper Dogs and gone to see Lenny to ask him about taking on a pup.

Patch looked up at Joe, wagged his tail and barked.

'You're right, Patch. I think it's nearly time to start.'

Lenny welcomed everyone and then asked Colonel Bates to say a few words. The senior-looking soldier went up on to the stage, followed by the soldier in the wheelchair and his dog.

'As you know, Helper Dogs has had links with the military services for over eight years now and we're very grateful to the Helper Dogs they've paired with some of our disabled servicemen and women.'

Then the soldier in the wheelchair spoke. 'My Helper Dog, Elmo, wakes me up in the morning as soon as the alarm goes off – or I should say usually two minutes before it's due, to be precise. He doesn't wear a watch, but he always knows exactly when it's time for me to get up.'

There was polite laughter at the soldier's joke. Joe watched as he reached down to stroke the head of the dog beside him. Then he carried on telling everyone more funny stories about his life with Elmo.

Joe looked over at his mum standing by the tea urn, ready to make drinks for people once the demonstration and talks were over. This was the reason they'd decided to look after a Helper Pup in the first place.

Joe and the other volunteers formed a line in preparation for their circle walk. Joe was glad he and Patch weren't the first ones to go on. Hamish and Olivia were.

'Meet Hamish and Olivia,' Lenny said into the microphone. 'Hamish is one of the few spaniels we've trained and he's heading off for his advanced training very shortly.'

Olivia and Hamish completed the circle and Lenny nodded at Joe, whose legs felt very wobbly.

'Come on, Patch.'

'Next I'd like to introduce you to Patch and Joe.'

Joe heard lots of *awwww*s from the audience as they slowly circled the room. He could almost hear, or at least he imagined he heard, his heart thumping, it was so loud. He was very, very nervous and didn't dare look up from the ground until they'd completed the circle.

Patch wasn't nervous at all and his tail wagged as he trotted beside Joe, looking at all the people who'd come to see him. His legs had grown faster than the rest of him in the past few weeks and he had a taller, almost gangly appearance now.

'Patch is nearly six months old and has been going into school with Joe. He even went to the beach with Joe's class,' Lenny said. 'Joe is the first under-sixteen-year-old we've had training a Helper Dog and we've all been very impressed with him and how well he and Patch have worked together.'

'That's really very good,' Joe heard someone in the audience say.

'Not many children of his age could do it,' said someone else.

Joe's face was burning with embarrassment and he longed for Lenny to stop talking about him.

He breathed a big sigh of relief when Lenny said, 'And now, Dora and Ann.'

The circle round the room had been bad enough, but the individual demonstrations were even worse. Joe was so anxious to get it right that he really did drop the pencil and Patch picked it up for him, only for Joe to drop it again by mistake. Patch wagged his tail as he pushed the pencil back into Joe's hand.

'This is very delicate work on Patch's part,' Lenny said. 'A pencil or a set of keys can be hard for a dog to pick up off the floor using just his mouth, but Patch is doing it admirably.'

Everyone clapped at the end of Patch's bit and Charlie whistled through her fingers even though Joe frowned to tell her to stop.

'Well done, very well done,' Joe heard Mr Humphreys say. 'Did I tell you that puppy lives next door?'

After the demonstrations there was a final circle of the dogs and their handlers and then it was all over, and Joe felt like he could finally breathe properly again.

Everyone wanted to congratulate him and give Patch a stroke or a pat.

'I hear your dad was in the military,' Colonel Bates said to Joe and his mum as everyone tucked into tea and cakes and dog biscuits.

Patch especially liked the peanut butter ones.

'Um, yes, sir,' answered Joe.

'Well, you're certainly doing a good job here and this fine chap is going to make the world of difference to someone's life one day.' He patted Patch's head.

'We're helping to train him in memory of Joe's dad,' said Mum as she handed the colonel a cup of tea.

'And a very fine tribute it is to his memory,' the colonel replied softly, and he nodded at Joe then moved on to talk to the other volunteers.

Patch sniffed and wagged his tail as Elmo and the soldier with him came to get their tea and dog biscuits.

'How long have you had Elmo for?' Mum asked him.

'Just over two years,' the soldier told her. 'Before he came along, everything looked pretty black and I couldn't see the point of even waking up each morning. He's made all the difference. And woe betide me if I don't get up and take him for a walk as soon as I'm awake.' He patted the dog and the dog licked his face. 'Yes, I'm talking about you, Elmo.'

'I'm so proud of little Patch,' Mrs Hodges said, coming over to them with Marnie once the soldier and Elmo had moved on. 'So very proud.'

Patch sniffed at Marnie and she nuzzled her face into his as if she were saying *well done* to her pup as well.

Joe felt very proud of Patch too. The puppy had worked so hard and was such a friendly dog.

'Here, Patch,' Charlie called to him and patted her lap. Patch ran over and put his paws on her lap so she could wrap her arms round his neck and hug him.

'You all did very well,' Lenny told the volunteers after everyone else had gone. 'Head Office was most impressed. So impressed with some of you, in fact, that they're thinking of bringing your assessments forward.'

Joe hoped Lenny wasn't talking about Patch because Joe didn't want him to go early. He wanted Patch to stay with him for as long as he possibly could.

'Thanks once again for all your hard work – and that ginger cake was delicious, Ann,' Lenny said, and Ann beamed. 'See you all at class on Wednesday.'

*

'Ready to go?' Joe's mum asked once the washing-up was done.

Joe nodded.

Patch was exhausted and Joe felt worn out too. It had been an amazing day, but he'd much rather not have to be on display in front of so many people again.

Lenny followed them out. 'The people from Head Office were really pleased with Patch. It won't be long before he's ready to go off for his final assessment and hopefully become a fully fledged Helper Dog,' he said as they were getting in the car. Patch wagged his tail as he accepted the treat, and the fuss Lenny made of him.

'How long before he has to leave?' Joe asked, swallowing hard.

'Difficult to say exactly. It depends on how many dogs they have to assess. But probably not before Christmas.' Patch nuzzled his hand for more treats and Lenny gave him another one. 'Go on then, but don't tell Ollie.'

They saw Mr Humphreys waiting at the bus stop.

'Can we give you a lift?' Joe's mum asked him, pulling in.

'Much appreciated,' Mr Humphreys said, climbing into the car. 'Can't stop thinking about those Helper Dogs. Jolly impressive indeed. Well done, Joe and Patch, and you too of course, Mary.'

'Thanks,' Joe mumbled, but he felt sick at the thought that Patch was going to be leaving.

When they got home, Patch stood up in his crate, which was rapidly becoming too small for him, and wagged his tail at Mr Humphreys and Joe.

Joe took a deep breath to steady himself as he unclipped the crate door. 'Good boy, Patch,' he said. 'You're such a good puppy,' and he pressed his face into Patch's fur and hugged him.

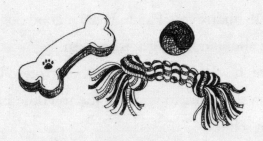

Chapter 22

Joe had taught Patch to pick up the post and bring it to him. But Joe was at school when the letter dropped through the letterbox, close to where Patch was lying at the front door, two weeks before the Christmas holidays started. Patch immediately jumped up and looked at the letter, then sat down, then stood up again and scratched at it with his paw until he could manage to get it in his mouth.

He took the letter upstairs to Joe's mum in her spare-bedroom office.

'Oh, thank you, Patch. What a good dog you are,' she said, taking it from him.

Patch wagged his tail and then trotted back down the stairs to wait for Joe to come home from school.

Joe knew something was wrong as soon as he walked in. Usually his mum was upstairs working in her office and only Patch was downstairs at the front door waiting for him. But today they were both there.

'What is it?' he asked.

Mum looked down at the letter she was holding. Joe looked at it too.

'What is it?' he repeated as she brushed away a tear that slipped down her face.

The letter was from Helper Dogs and Mum read it out to Joe.

' "We would like to thank you for all your hard work in helping to turn Patch into the wonderful puppy he is today," ' she read. ' "It is now time for him to continue on his journey to becoming a Helper Dog and changing someone's life forever. Patch's assessment will take place on the twentieth of December. He will be needed at the Helper Dogs headquarters the day before the assessment. Please ensure Patch is ready. He should bring with him his crate and bedding, food and water bowls, his Helper Dogs jacket, a toy and possibly a ball. (Please don't send more than one toy as we simply don't have space for them and they will be disposed of.)

' "Thanks once again for all your dedication. Helper Dogs could not exist without its magnificent dog-loving volunteers. We would like to invite you to our Christmas celebration for dogs in advanced training on the twenty-fourth of December." '

Patch looked up at her and whined.

'Helper Dogs.' Joe took the letter from her and read it again. 'They're taking him away. Before Christmas?' he said, stunned.

He'd been dreading Christmas already, but at least they'd have had Patch with them. But now it had turned into the absolute worst time of the year.

'And they want us to come and celebrate.'

He didn't feel like celebrating, not one little bit. Although it'd mean he'd see Patch and he definitely did want to do that.

Patch put his paw out to him.

'It's OK,' Joe told the puppy bravely, although he was almost shaking. Joe knew Patch was really good at picking up on emotions and he didn't want to alarm him. 'It's OK. Where's your ball? Let's go outside and play.'

Knowing that Patch might one day be his Helper Dog had kept Sam going through months of operations and physiotherapy. If he didn't keep going and get as fit as he could, Patch would be given to someone else. It was as simple as that.

Late at night, when he couldn't sleep, he'd look at Patch's online diary, although he'd read it all a thousand times already.

'I love the bit where Patch learnt to swim,' he told the night nurse as he showed her the photographs Joe had taken. 'But he wasn't too sure about crabs!' Thinking about Patch and those crabs always made him smile.

But now he knew he could be living with Patch very soon.

The army occupational therapist had come to talk to him about the flat that was to be specially adapted for him.

'It has to have as large a garden as possible,' he'd said. 'I want Patch to have space to play. I want to watch him run down the garden after a ball.'

Most of the rehabilitation flats had small gardens so they'd be easier to maintain, but the occupational therapist had finally found one at the end of a block she thought might be suitable.

'Perfect!' Sam had said when he'd seen it.

'It's an older flat and not as well decorated as some of the others,' the occupational therapist had said.

But Sam didn't care about decor.

'That's a garden a dog can have fun in,' he'd said. 'It's just right.'

The occupational therapist had smiled. 'Then we'll start getting it adapted for you,' she'd said.

'I need to be in it before Christmas,' Sam had told her. 'Patch is being assessed on the twentieth of December.'

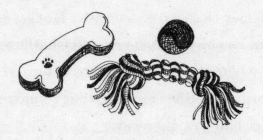

Chapter 23

Christmas was only three weeks away. Which meant that there was just over two weeks before Patch's assessment. Joe wanted to make those weeks the most fun for Patch that he possibly could.

He didn't want to tell anyone Patch was leaving. It felt somehow that if he didn't say it out loud, then it might not really be real.

But his mum told Mr Humphreys when they were putting out the dustbins.

'I'll miss the little imp,' he said. 'Place won't be the same without him.'

Helper Dogs wrote to let Mrs Hodges know about Patch's achievement and Charlie found out when she bumped into Lenny at the supermarket. She came speeding round in her wheelchair straight away.

'I can't believe he's going,' she said as she stroked Patch. 'I'll miss him so much.' She had tears in her eyes when she looked up at Joe. 'You have to bring Patch into school this week so everyone can say goodbye to him. You have to. It wouldn't be fair if you didn't. We all love him.'

Charlie was right. 'I will,' Joe said softly, and he brought Patch into school for two days rather than his usual one.

Miss Addams gave them an extended break and let the children take Patch out on to the sports field at the back of the school.

'I so wish Patch didn't have to go away,' said Charlie.

But no one could wish it as much as Joe did.

*

On the last day of term, Joe's class had a small party for Patch. Callum and Daniel bought Patch a ball and Miss Addams gave him a packet of dog treats.

'I wasn't sure which would be best, but the secretary said he really liked these ones.'

Patch wagged his tail as she showed him the treats. He wasn't sure what was going on, but he liked all the fuss everyone was making of him.

Joe felt like his heart was breaking.

Charlie brought in a small savoury cake she'd made for Patch.

'I found the recipe on the Internet,' she said. 'They've got loads of recipes for dog treats on there. This one's got cheese in it.'

In the playground everyone wanted to give Patch one last stroke and in assembly the head teacher told them all, 'Today is probably the last time little Patch will be visiting us and I'm sure we'll all be sad not to see his waggy tail or hear his bark any more, but Patch is now going to carry on with his training to be a Helper Dog.'

He might come back, Joe thought, and he wished with all his heart that Patch would fail his assessment, even though he knew it was wrong to wish it. Sam needed Patch. But if Patch failed the assessment he'd get to stay with Joe forever.

Once school was over for the term, Joe spent all his time with Patch.

Callum and Daniel and Archie came with him and Patch to the park. They threw the ball Callum and Daniel had bought for the pup to run after, and raced around with him as his tail wagged and wagged.

'He has to be the best puppy ever,' Callum said as they all collapsed on a bench, exhausted, and Joe couldn't agree more.

At the supermarket the manager gave Patch one of the special Christmas stockings filled with dog treats and a toy.

'We'll all miss not seeing his furry face around here any more,' he said to Joe, and Joe nodded. They couldn't miss his furry face as much as he was going to.

On the Saturday Joe and his mum and Charlie took Patch to the Christmas night market. Patch sniffed at the different new smells and Charlie sniffed too.

'Roasted chestnuts,' she said.

They didn't give Patch any chestnuts, but he got to taste a bit of Christmas cheese.

'Swallowed in an instant,' smiled Joe's mum.

And then Patch got to taste some Christmas sausage from another stall.

'Was that good?' Joe asked him as Patch looked up at him, wagged his tail, then put out his paw to ask for more.

'Try this,' a stallholder said to Charlie, offering her some bratwurst.

'Thanks,' Charlie said, and she gave it to Patch.

'Not too much,' Joe's mum warned. 'Even though I know he likes it.'

Patch ducked behind Joe's legs as they went past the man dressed as Father Christmas who rang a clanging bell and said 'Ho ho ho'.

'Not too sure about him,' Joe said, patting the pup.

Back at home Patch fell fast asleep in front of the fire, full of all the food and the sights and sounds he'd experienced, while Joe sat beside him and stroked his soft fur.

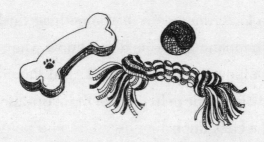

Chapter 24

On the morning of the eighteenth of December Joe woke to find everything felt quieter, and the light in his bedroom wasn't quite the same as usual. He got out of bed and pulled back the curtains. A thick layer of snow covered the garden.

'Yes!'

He'd been hoping for days that it would snow. He grabbed a coat to wear over his pyjamas and pulled on his wellingtons. Patch jumped off the bed, his tail wagging. He knew from Joe's excitement that something thrilling was happening, but he didn't know what.

'Come on, Patch!' he said, and Patch ran after him as Joe pelted down the stairs and out of the back door.

Patch came to a stop at the doorstep and for a second just looked at the strange new white stuff that covered his garden.

'Come on, Patch!' Joe called to him again, and he grabbed handfuls of the white stuff and threw it up in the air.

If Joe wasn't scared of it, then Patch wasn't either. He ran out, lifting his paws high at the shock of the cold on his puppy pads.

Joe made a snowball, throwing it across the white garden, and Patch ran after it. When he reached it he sniffed at the snowball, gave it a lick and then sneezed with excitement. Then he ran round and round the garden, kicking up sprays of snow before he rolled over and over in it, getting himself covered in ice crystals as Joe laughed.

Joe ran inside and grabbed his dad's camera from the kitchen table and took picture after picture of the puppy.

'Joe, come on in – you two must be frozen by now,' his mum called an hour later.

Inside the house Joe drank a steamy mug of hot chocolate and Patch had a dog chew and a long drink of water before they headed back out again as soon as Joe had got properly dressed. Patch brought Squeaker down the stairs and took the toy out into the snow with him.

When they came back in again Mum had put on some Christmas music. 'Felt right, what with all the snow,' she smiled.

They'd put up their greetings cards, but hadn't done much in the way of decorations.

The real fir tree they'd always had before had been replaced by a small gold artificial one that was waiting to be unpacked from its box.

'Pancakes for breakfast?' Mum offered. Pancakes were Joe's favourite.

As a special treat Patch had a small amount of chicken with his breakfast. Helper Dogs only provided dry food for their dogs. Patch thought the chicken was very fine and Joe's mum gave him a little more.

'There you go – eat it slowly or you won't even taste it.' But *chicken* and *slow* were two words that didn't go together as far as Patch was concerned.

After breakfast they took the artificial tree out of the box along with the packet of decorations that came with it.

Joe laughed as Patch tried to squeeze himself inside the empty box.

'That's not a dog crate.'

Mum helped to put the baubles on the branches of the tree.

'It's not the same,' Joe said.

'It'll never be the same,' agreed Joe's mum, giving him a hug.

'We'll never forget Dad.'

'No, we won't.'

Joe felt very close to tears. 'And we'll never forget Patch either.'

'Never.'

The doorbell rang and Patch ran to see who it was. He wagged his tail when he saw his friend from next door.

'Been baking,' Mr Humphreys said, holding out a tray of mince pies and two star-shaped biscuits. 'The stars are for your little star there. Got a bit of chicken in them.'

'How kind,' said Mum. 'Come in.'

'Can't stay long,' said Mr Humphreys, sitting down in an armchair. 'Just wanted to say goodbye to this little chap and bring him something tasty. He's going to leave a big hole in everyone's hearts when he's gone.' Patch rested his head on Mr Humphreys' knee and looked up as the old man stroked him.

'I'd have brought him a toy, but you said he could only take one with him.'

'His favourite toy's this one,' Joe said, going to pick up a snow-covered Squeaker from the garden.

'It'll dry before tomorrow,' Mum said.

All day long Joe and his mum did everything they possibly could to make Patch's last day with them really special. They didn't talk to each other about how much they'd miss Patch because it didn't need to be said. They both knew if they were sad it would make Patch sad too, so they concentrated on making his day fun instead.

After lunch Joe and his mum made a snow-man while Patch ran around and barked at it.

'He should have a snowdog too,' Joe decided, and he started pressing more snow together. 'Every snowman should have a snowdog.'

Joe stayed out in the garden with Patch long after it got dark, until finally his mum came out and said it really was time to go to bed.

That night Patch lay next to Joe on his bed, fast asleep and snoring softly. But Joe couldn't sleep. Tomorrow Patch would be gone and nothing would be the same without him there.

Outside it started to rain, turning the white snow to greyish slush. Joe looked out to see that the snowman and snowdog had already started turning to mush.

Joe picked up his laptop and added a few photos of Patch in the snow to the online diary. This was probably going to be the last time he wrote Patch's diary for him.

Today my garden was covered with cold white wet stuff called snow. Joe and me played in it for hours

and hours. Joe's mum helped to make a snowdog,
although it didn't look much like me.

Joe added the photo of Patch sniffing at the snowdog. He looked over at Patch as he twitched in his sleep. Today had been a very special day. A day he'd never ever forget. A tear rolled down Joe's face and he brushed it away with his fingers.

I'm looking forward to tomorrow and more adventures
with Sam . . .

Joe typed.

Sam saw the photos almost immediately and smiled at Patch's snowy face. Tomorrow he was leaving the hospital. Tomorrow everything was going to change.

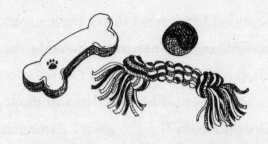

Chapter 25

The next morning Patch woke Joe up by licking his face. He was ready for more snowy adventures. But there was no snow left.

Lenny arrived at ten o'clock to take Patch and Joe in the Helper Dogs van to the Helper Dogs headquarters to drop Patch off for his test the next day.

'It'll be good for you to see where Patch'll be sleeping before his final assessment tomorrow,' Lenny said. 'I think you'll be impressed with the place.'

Joe didn't know what to say. He felt so many things all at once. He knew he should be excited and happy for Patch, and want him to do well in his assessment, but all he felt was empty.

'Does he really have to go in his crate in the back?' Joe asked Lenny. 'Can't he come next to me just this once?'

'It is safest in the crate,' Lenny said.

Joe sighed. He didn't want to be even a few centimetres away from Patch during the journey. 'Can I go in the back with him then?'

'Go on.'

Joe's mum came out to say goodbye. She gave Patch one last hug and tucked Squeaker into his crate with him. She then gave Joe a quick hug too and whispered in his ear, 'He's going to be just fine. And so are you,' before quickly turning away.

Joe sat in the back with Patch and stroked him through the bars of his crate. Patch whimpered and licked Joe's hand, telling him as clearly as he could that he didn't like being in the crate and wanted to come out.

After only a few minutes, Joe felt the van come to a stop. They couldn't be there already. It wasn't time to say goodbye yet, was it?

'I'm just popping in to see Riley,' Lenny shouted through to Joe. 'He's been out for the first time and is playing with other dogs again. Won't be a minute,' Lenny called as he got out.

Joe opened Patch's crate door so he could give him a proper stroke rather than just touching him through the bars with his fingers, but he didn't let Patch get out. His fur was puppy soft.

Patch nestled his head into Joe's hand and Joe swallowed hard.

'It's going to be OK,' he told the puppy. 'You might not even pass the assessment.' He sniffed and Patch looked up at him with his big brown eyes. He could sense his friend was sad, very sad, and that something was wrong, but he didn't know what it was. He gave a whine.

Joe sniffed again. He knew in his heart of hearts that Patch was bound to pass his assessment. He was so smart and so quick to learn things and eager to please. He wouldn't understand why he couldn't be with Joe any more. And what about when it came to saying goodbye? Patch might think he'd done something wrong. He wouldn't know he had to leave Joe because he'd done so many things right and had been such a good dog. This was probably the last day that Patch would be his puppy. Suddenly Joe just couldn't bear it. He could feel tears coming and he didn't want Patch to see him upset, not today.

Patch whined and pawed at the crate as Joe closed the metal door again.

And the next thing Joe knew, he was out of the van and running down the street, not knowing where he was going, but just needing to run and run.

Inside the van Patch was confused. Why had Joe left him behind? He barked to let Joe know he'd forgotten to take him with him. His bark sounded strange as it echoed inside the metal box. He didn't like the sound, but he barked again and again, over and over. He tried to push his paws through the bars and scraped his claws on the side of his crate. He whined, then barked again.

'All right, all right,' said Lenny's voice a few minutes later. 'What on earth's going on back there?'

He opened the back doors of the van.

'Where's Joe gone?' He looked around and waited for him to come back, but the boy was nowhere to be seen.

*

Joe ran until he couldn't run any more. He didn't know this part of town and he wasn't sure where he was. His phone rang, but he ignored it. He didn't want to talk to anyone at all.

Mr Humphreys was on the bus when he saw Joe running along the street towards the centre of town. He pressed the button and got off at the next stop.

'Whoa there. What's wrong?' he said as he caught up with Joe.

Joe gasped and gulped down air, trying to be brave, trying not to cry.

'I was supposed to go with him and now I've let him down.'

'Calm down, son. Tell me what's happened. Why aren't you with Patch?'

'I just couldn't bear saying goodbye to someone . . . again.'

'Hardest thing in the world,' Mr Humphreys said.

'What is?' Joe asked, dashing away his tears before Mr Humphreys could see them.

'Losing someone you love,' Mr Humphreys said softly, and Joe realized Mr Humphreys truly did understand how he felt.

'Yes, it is.'

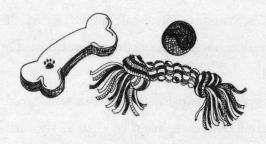

Chapter 26

Patch still sat up waiting for Joe to come back as Lenny started the engine. But sitting up in the small crate wasn't comfortable, so he lay down. Joe wasn't there to stroke him any more and all he could see was the interior of the Helper Dogs van. Finally he dozed, but didn't fall asleep.

A while later the van came to a juddery halt.

'Here we are at last,' said Lenny. He came round to the back of the van and opened the doors. Patch was already sitting up with a paw resting on the bars of his crate.

'Yes, you can come out now,' Lenny said as he pulled back the bolt and clipped on Patch's lead.

It was dark outside and the air smelt different to what Patch was used to. It was the smell of the countryside.

'Thought you two could do with this,' a voice called to them.

'Hello there, thanks for waiting for us,' Lenny said as the kennel maid, Emma, came over to them with a mug of coffee and a sandwich for Lenny and a bowl of water and some food for Patch.

Patch was very hungry and he wolfed all the food down and was then given a long stroke and a cuddle by his new friend. He could smell other dogs, lots of other dogs that he didn't know, and one dog that he did. He sniffed the air and his tail thumped on the ground.

'Who've we got with us from your centre, Lenny?' Emma asked him.

'Hamish should still be here, I think,' Lenny replied.

'Oh yes, the lovely spaniel. Come on, Patch. Let's take you to see your friend.'

Hamish, like the other dogs in the kennels, was in a small room with a dog sofa in one corner and a dog bed on the floor. There was also a water bowl and a blanket and a toy. Hamish immediately ran over to see them all, his tail wagging.

Patch wagged his tail back and sniffed at the other dog.

'You'll be OK here now you've got a doggy friend,' Emma told Patch, and she put Patch into Hamish's room with him.

'It'll be nice for Hamish to have some company too,' she told Lenny.

'I'll be back to check on you both in a bit,' Emma said to Patch and Hamish. 'If you settle down nicely together, then Patch can stay with you for the night, Hamish. But if you're playing all the time and neither of you are getting any sleep, then I'll have to put Patch in a separate kennel.'

Lenny smiled as he looked at Patch. He was close to the edge of the dog room with his head tilted to one side as if he were listening to Emma's every word.

'You be a good pup now,' Lenny said as he crouched down and put his fingers through the bars to stroke him. 'I'm glad he's got Hamish to keep him company. He'll be missing his volunteer parent Joe, and heaven knows how much Joe must be missing him, poor lad. He's only a boy. I thought he understood that Patch would be leaving him one day but . . .'

'Too hard to comprehend until they're gone,' Emma said.

'Yes,' agreed Lenny, 'but Joe only recently lost his dad too. Maybe we shouldn't have signed him up to the programme. Poor lad was on his way with me here today, but then he ran off. All too much for him.'

Lenny had spoken to Joe's mum to check that Joe had got home safely. He was pleased to hear the boy had been brought back by the old man Mr Humphreys. Thank goodness he'd found him. But now Lenny phoned Joe's mum again.

'He won't speak to you, Lenny,' Joe's mum said. 'I'm sorry but he's taking this very hard.'

'That's OK,' Lenny told her. 'Can you just tell him that Patch is at headquarters now and he's bunking with his friend Hamish?'

'It's like puppy sleepover time in the kennel sometimes and no sleep's happening,' Emma told Lenny ruefully as she saw him back to his van.

'Patch should be tuckered out, poor little mite. It's always tough letting them go,' Lenny said.

'But worth it when you see the difference they can make,' Emma said.

Lenny nodded.

By the time Emma came back from waving Lenny off, Patch was fast asleep on Hamish's bed. Hamish wasn't asleep, but was watching over his friend from the sofa.

Later that night Patch whimpered in his sleep and cried out. Hamish's bed didn't smell the same as Joe's, and Joe's bed was where Patch had always slept at night. He half woke up and then drifted back to sleep. It had been a very long day.

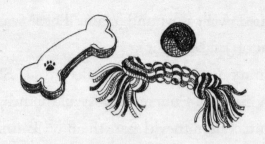

Chapter 27

The next morning Patch woke up and immediately ran to the side of the kennel room to see if Joe was there. He barked to let him know where he was, but lots of other dogs – at least ten of them – were also barking.

'All right, all right, I'm coming,' Emma said.

Once Emma had checked all the dogs were OK from the night before, more kennel staff arrived to take the dogs for a walk. Louis took Hamish and Emma took Patch.

As they walked, Patch kept looking around as if he were searching for something, and he whined every now and again. There was no scent of Joe here.

Emma understood what was wrong. She'd seen this behaviour in almost all of the dogs before. Once they'd had their walk Emma gave Patch his breakfast. It was the same food that Joe had given him every day. He was missing Joe, but he was still hungry and gobbled it all up.

'Slow down there,' Emma said. 'You don't want to choke.'

Later in the afternoon, after Patch had had a whole morning of being with Hamish and was getting a bit bored, Emma took him to be assessed.

The assessor tested Patch on basic obedience and learning new skills, whether he could think for himself and how he handled stressful situations and obstacles.

Patch passed his test with flying colours.

'Well done, Patch,' Emma said as she stroked him. Patch knew he'd done well and kept wagging his tail and stepping from one foot to the other with excitement.

'Whoever he was with before us did a fine job,' the assessor said.

Emma looked down at the paperwork she had for Patch.

'Oh, he was with Joe – the boy who did that amazing diary all about him.'

The assessor nodded; he'd seen it too. 'I loved all those photos he took of him.'

'Me too.'

Sam had been waiting by the phone all day and it only rang once before he answered it.

'Yes?'

'Would you like to meet your new Helper Dog?' the assessor asked him.

Sam breathed out a sigh of relief. Patch had passed. It was time for them to meet and the first part of their team training together to begin.

'Yes. Yes, I would,' he said.

'Then we'll see you tomorrow for the start of your residential stay.'

Sam was so excited to be meeting Patch at last that he arrived hours too early.

'It's only seven o'clock,' Emma said. 'You'll have an awfully long wait.'

But Sam told her he didn't care about that.

When Patch was finally brought into the room, Sam called softly to him.

'Patch, Patch!'

And Patch looked straight at him with his big brown eyes.

Sam swallowed hard. The pup was even more special than Sam had imagined. Patch tilted his head to one side as if he were weighing Sam up.

'Patch!' Sam called again and patted his lap. Patch came bounding over to him.

Sam stroked the pup and Patch put his front paws on Sam's lap so it was easier for the soldier to reach him. Sam buried his face in Patch's soft fur and Patch licked away the salty water that ran down his face.

'Looks as though Patch likes you,' Emma said.

Sam nodded. 'Yes, it does,' he said, his voice cracking.

'Now the hard work begins,' Emma told him. 'Over the next two weeks, during your residential stay here, we'll be teaching Patch the tasks that would be most helpful specifically for you.'

'If he could drag my ceiling hoist to me to help me pull myself up out of bed in the mornings, that'd be great. My arms aren't as strong as I'd like them to be yet.'

'No problem,' Emma said. 'Patch will be able to do those things and more to assist you in no time.'

Patch wagged his tail and barked.

'Looks like he's ready to learn,' laughed Sam as he bent down to stroke the pup. He was hardly able to believe that Patch was really going to be his Helper Dog. He'd wanted it for so long.

'You'll need to take him out for walks,' Emma said. 'To burn off all that excess puppy energy.'

'Of course.'

'In all weathers.'

'Looking forward to it.'

Emma smiled. She was sure Sam and Patch were a perfect match.

'After your residential stay here there will be a ninety-day probation period to make sure you're a perfect fit for each other.'

'We will be,' Sam said.

'Your residential stay's over Christmas and we always have a bit of a do for the dogs, handlers and past puppy raisers. We've already asked Joe and his mum. Did you know that

Joe's dad was a soldier too? He was killed on duty back in May.'

'No, I didn't,' Sam said, looking up. 'But I'd really like to meet Joe, more than ever now. I'm so grateful to him and his mother for all their hard work in training Patch. And for letting him move on to come and live with me.'

'Come on, I'll show you your room – yours and Patch's!' said Emma.

Later that day, while Patch had a snooze, Sam opened his laptop and went to Patch's diary page.

I've been waiting to meet Patch for so long that I could hardly breathe when we met for the first time today. Just having him with me is going to make all the difference in the world to my life now. I'm so grateful to you, Joe, and would like to shake your hand. Please do come to the Helper Dogs party on the 24th. Patch would be over the moon to see you and so would I.

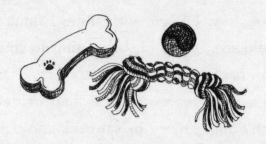

Chapter 28

Joe lay on his bed looking at the ceiling. He could hear his mum in the room next door typing on the computer. The house felt completely different without Patch there. They were so used to his waggy tail greeting them when they came through the front door, his soft furry body lying next to them and his head pushing its way under their hands when he wanted a stroke. It suddenly felt very empty and quiet.

Joe's mum popped her head round his bedroom door.

'Joe, love, I've got something I think you should see,' she said, beckoning to him to follow her back into her home office.

When Joe read what Sam had written in Patch's online diary, he sat back and sighed. He could feel his mum watching him. He took a deep breath.

'I think we should go,' he said to her, and she immediately knew that Joe was talking about the party at the Helper Dogs headquarters.

'I think we should too,' she said. 'As long as you're sure.'

'I'd like to meet Sam and I'd like to know . . . I'd like to know that Patch will be happy.'

'Well, I think you'll have lots of support too. I can think of a few other people who might like to come with us. Helper Dogs said all Patch's friends are welcome.'

Joe smiled and reached for his phone to call Charlie, while his mum popped next door to tell Mr Humphreys.

When Charlie heard they were going, she wanted to come to the party too and she told everyone she met about it.

Mrs Hodges had already been invited by Helper Dogs as she'd donated Patch to them.

The next morning Joe, his mum and Mr Humphreys all set off together.

'I'm looking forward to seeing the little imp again. Feels like weeks instead of days since I've seen him,' Mr Humphreys said.

Joe and his mum exchanged a look in the car mirror. It had felt like years to them. They were almost bursting to see Patch.

At last they arrived and pulled into the car park. Helper Dogs headquarters consisted of an old manor house where the offices were located, a large modern dog-kennel block and training area, and three fields surrounding it for exercising the dogs in.

'Hello, you must be Joe and Mrs Scott,' Emma said when she met them at the entrance.

'Please, call me Mary. And this is our neighbour Mr Humphreys. He and Patch are good friends too.'

'We have this party every year,' Emma told Joe and his mum and Mr Humphreys. 'And every year it gets bigger with so many different people coming whose lives have been affected by a Helper Dog. It's my absolute favourite event that we have.'

As she led them into the hall where the party was being held, Joe looked over at the huge real fir tree in the corner of the room that reached up to the ceiling and was decorated with lights and tinsel and baubles. His dad had loved big trees. This one even had presents underneath it.

'Dog presents,' Emma told him when she saw Joe looking at the tree. 'And not only do we have presents under the tree, the dogs have their own Christmas stockings for Santa to fill too.'

Joe grinned. 'Do you think Patch'll like his first Christmas dinner turkey?'

'I've never known a dog that doesn't,' Emma said, smiling back at him.

Patch wasn't the only dog currently at Helper Dogs headquarters for his residential advanced training. There was also Hamish, who'd been placed with an ex-pilot called Sheila, plus two Labradors, called Faber and Winnie, and all of them had friends and family at the party too. Also many of the Helper Dogs administrative staff had brought in their own pets for the day.

There were so many people and dogs inside the hall there was hardly room to move.

Joe felt a tap on his shoulder.

'Charlie said everyone who knew Patch was welcome,' Callum and Daniel grinned. 'This party is excellent.'

'I had to say goodbye to him,' said Joe's teacher Miss Addams.

'He felt like part of the school,' agreed Mr Potter, his head teacher.

Archie and his mum came over with Ben. Joe saw Sheila going past wearing a tinsel necklace.

'But how did you all know about the party?' he asked.

'A little bird told us,' said Miss Addams, nodding over Joe's shoulder. He turned round to see Charlie and her dad across the other side of the hall, patting Hamish and laughing. She caught his eye, gave him a big smile and then headed over to join them.

Joe couldn't believe everyone had come. All these people who loved Patch too. Joe wished for the millionth time that his dad could have met Patch. He knew he'd have loved him just like everyone else who met him did.

'Do you think Dad knows about Patch?' he whispered to his mum.

'I'm sure he does,' she said as she lightly squeezed his hand. 'And he'd be so very proud of you and all the training you did with him.'

Mr Humphreys nodded.

But Joe shook his head. 'Patch was really easy to train,' he said. 'Just about taught himself!'

'That's what Little Blue did,' Mrs Hodges said, overhearing Joe and his mum and talking to Mr Humphreys. 'That's Patch's sister, you know. Only she taught herself to do lots of things her new owners didn't want her to do, like chewing cushions and chasing cats. They said they'd decided a dog wasn't for them after all and so she's being returned to me after Christmas. I couldn't let her go to an animal shelter.'

'My dog Billy used to chew the cushions when he first came to us. But once I'd told him "no" a few times and gave him something else to chew instead he stopped doing it. Pups want to be good but it's hard for them to always know how to behave if we don't show them.'

Mrs Hodges nodded. 'Billy's lucky to have you,' she said. 'How old is he?'

'Oh, sorry. Billy's long gone. He'd be almost forty years old by now,' Mr Humphreys said. 'Still miss him, though, and even more so since I've met young Patch.'

'Can't Little Blue be a Helper Pup like Patch?' Charlie asked.

'If she's at all like she was when she was living with me, she can be very wilful at times . . .' Mrs Hodges warned.

Charlie grinned at that one. 'Sounds just like me.'

'I'm not at all sure she'd be ideal,' Mrs Hodges said, shaking her head. She looked at Mr Humphreys. 'What Little Blue could really do with is some stability.'

'Oh, I'm sorry to hear that,' Mr Humphreys said. 'I bet Patch's sister could make a really good Helper Dog too. Especially if she had someone like Joe raising her.'

'Maybe,' Mrs Hodges said, looking at Mr Humphreys thoughtfully.

'Perhaps . . .' Mr Humphreys said, but at that moment the room immediately hushed when Meera Callum, the head of Helper Dogs, wheeled herself out on to the stage at the far end of the room near the Christmas tree.

'Thank you so much for coming. I'd like you all to give a big hand to our dogs in advanced training that are spending the holiday with us this year,' she said.

First to join her on the stage was Hamish and his new partner, then the two Labs with theirs. Joe realized he'd been holding his breath, and exhaled as Patch and Sam finally came out too.

Sam was in a motorized wheelchair and Patch trotted along beside him, his tail wagging as he looked up at Sam every now and again.

'Where's Joe?' Sam asked, and everyone who knew him looked round at Joe.

Joe felt even more embarrassed than at the open day.

'I never knew your dad,' Sam said from the stage, 'but I know he must have been a good man for you and your mum to have done something so amazing in memory of him.'

Joe watched as Patch put his head under Sam's hand and Sam stroked him. Mum was squeezing Joe's hand so hard that she was hurting him, but he didn't mind. He understood. If she hadn't been squeezing his hand so hard he'd probably have been squeezing hers.

Sam continued. 'I know Patch is going to change my life in a thousand ways for the better and every day – every hour, in fact – that I'm with him I want to thank you.'

Patch suddenly went still. He'd spotted Joe in the centre of the hall. The next moment he'd jumped off the stage and was bounding over to him.

'As I said, I never knew your dad,' Sam went on as Patch found Joe, and Joe hugged the puppy to him. 'But I know he would have been proud of what you've done.'

But Joe didn't feel proud of himself and his mum; he felt proud of Patch and all that he'd become.

Everyone in the hall started to clap as Sam left the stage and headed over to Joe.

Joe hugged and hugged Patch. He could still see the tiny little pup that he'd once been, but now Patch was starting a new life as a real Helper Dog with Sam.

'Would you mind if I carry on with his online diary?' Sam asked as he reached Joe. 'I'd tell it from Patch's point of view like you did.'

'That'd be great,' Joe said. Then he'd always know how Patch was, and it'd be like he hadn't totally gone.

'He learnt so much and so fast when he was with you, it would amaze me reading all about it in the diary,' Sam said. 'And now he's got even more to learn. I always tell everyone I meet what a hero he is. He's already done so much for me. He's my hero pup and I know my life would be much less of a life without him in it.'

Sam shook Joe's hand and at that moment Joe knew he'd done the right thing, even though it was the hardest thing he'd ever had to do.

'Time to go,' Joe's mum said softly. 'It's a long journey back.'

'Keep in touch,' Sam said.

Joe nodded and crouched down for one last hug with Patch.

As they left the room, Joe looked back and saw Patch gazing after him. Patch wagged his tail and then turned back to Sam.

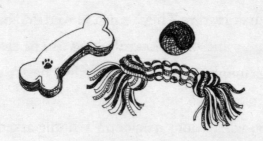

Epilogue

Just over two weeks later, Joe was reading Patch's online diary when Charlie came round with a New Year present for him and his mum balanced on her lap.

'They're to go outside,' she told them as Joe opened the parcel and found a set of wind chimes inside. 'They bring good luck.'

Charlie went into the back garden with Joe to help him find a suitable spot for them.

'How's Patch doing?'

'Brilliantly,' Joe told her. 'He and Sam are out and about to the park or the woods just about every day. They've just moved into Sam's flat now and Sam bought a dog bed as Helper Dogs told him to, but so far Patch hasn't slept in it once.'

'So where does he sleep?' Charlie asked.

Joe grinned. Only someone without a dog would ask that.

'On Sam's bed.'

'Oh, I'd like to have a dog to sleep on my bed too. Lenny says it won't be much longer before I get my own Helper Pup. I can't wait . . . What's that?'

They both looked round at the sound of barking. It was coming from behind Mr Humphreys' hedge.

Joe's mum brought them out some hot chocolate.

'Mum, I think Mr Humphreys might have a dog in his garden,' Joe told her.

'Oh, I don't think that can be right,' Joe's mum said doubtfully.

'It is,' said Charlie. 'Mr Humphreys! Mr Humphreys! Have you got a dog?' she shouted over the fence.

'Come round and you'll see!' Mr Humphreys called back.

'We'll be right there.'

It took them less than a minute to ring the doorbell, but it took a long time for Mr Humphreys to open his front door. There was a lot of what Joe and Charlie knew could only be barking coming from inside the house.

'Hush, now,' Joe could hear Mr Humphreys saying. 'Good girl – sit. Now wait.'

Mr Humphreys finally opened the door. His face looked much redder than usual, but he was smiling.

'There's someone I'd like you all to say hello to,' he said, opening the door wider so Charlie could steer her wheelchair inside.

Charlie gave a little yelp and Joe gasped.

Sitting on Mr Humphreys' carpet was Little Blue. She had managed to sit and wait until Mr Humphreys had opened the door. But it was impossible for her to do so for even a second longer and she jumped up, wagging her tail, as Joe and Charlie rushed in.

'Charlie, meet Little Blue, or LB as I like to call her,' Mr Humphreys said. 'She already knows Joe.'

'She's so cute,' Charlie grinned as she patted her lap and LB put her paws on it.

Joe remembered her being the smallest of Marnie's litter. She was still smaller than Patch now, but not by much.

'But I don't understand . . .' Joe started to say.

'Well, Mrs Hodges and I were chatting at the Helper Dogs party and she told me Little Blue needed a new home. Didn't work out so well with her first owners. They realized a puppy was too much work for them after all.

Anyway, it got me to thinking . . . Now, I'm not as young as I used to be,' Mr Humphreys said, looking at Joe. 'And she's got an awful lot of energy. So I'll need some help walking her and taking her to classes. What do you think?'

Joe remembered how much Patch and his little sister had loved each other, and spent hours playing together, and curled up close to sleep when they were tiny pups.

Little Blue wasn't Patch, and he could never feel the same about any other puppy as he'd done about him. But he thought Patch would be happy if he helped her, and he was sure she'd love learning new things just as much as Patch had done.

Joe looked at Charlie and up at his mum, who both smiled back at him.

'We'll help,' he said as he stroked Little Blue, and Charlie nodded. He'd like to do that for Patch, his hero pup.

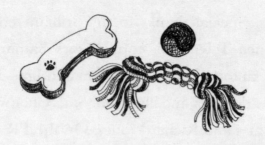

Acknowledgements

Researching and meeting different assistance dogs and the people who work with them for this book has been an absolute pleasure. I've been constantly amazed at the variety of helpful things dogs can do for people and would like to thank the humans I met for generously giving of their time to answer my endless questions, and the dogs for allowing me to make a fuss of them.

I've been very lucky to work with most of the same wonderful dog-loving team from Puffin on this book as I have for my previous ones. Special thanks to my brilliant editor Anthea Townsend, copy-editors Samantha Mackintosh, Mary O'Riordan and Jane Tait, cover designer and illustrator Sara Chadwick-Holmes and Richard Jones. On the PR side there's been Rhiannon Winfield and Jessica Farrugia-Sharples, marketing manager Gemma Green, and sales whizzes Tineke Mollemans and Kirsty Bradbury.

Not forgetting my super smart agent Clare Pearson at Eddison Pearson who I've worked with for most of my writing career.

I'd also like to thank the many booksellers, bookclubs, librarians and teachers who've been such advocates of the books. Bedford Waterstone's even provided a dog bodyguard for Traffy when she was being swamped by schoolchildren on my last book tour.

The letters and emails I've had from children about the books have been a joy to read. One I particularly liked was written by Rebecca, PJ,

Bo and Kai from The Vine School. Two of them are now seriously thinking of becoming dog trainers when they grow up and I wish them all the best. Most of the emails I receive ask questions about Traffy and Bella and the assistance-dog puppies I've worked with. I hope this book gives a few answers.

Lenny's dog school owes a big thanks to Happy Dog in Bedfordshire where Traffy and Bella both went to pre-puppy and puppy classes, joined in agility courses, and took their Kennel Club exams and made lots of friends (as did I).

Many of the dogs we met there had come from dog-rescue centres. These dogs had been lucky enough to find a second home after their first one hadn't worked out. Dog-rescue and rehoming centres receive lots and lots of puppies that are no longer wanted just after Christmas, which is very sad. Having a dog is a big commitment but one that is a joy if it's carefully thought through first.

Finally, special thanks as always must go to my dear husband and our own two dogs, Traffy and Bella, who've happily come along to different dog charity fêtes and fun days as part of my research. For the past year Traffy's been visiting a local school as a reading therapy dog, listening to children read. Judging by how she pulls me into the school as soon as we arrive, I'd say she very much enjoys going, and the school has reported significant improvements amongst Traffy's readers.

Bella has come out on stage at a few of my speaking engagements, but truthfully she prefers playing with her ball and swimming in the river.

They both inspire me in a thousand ways every day.

  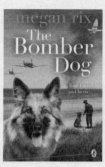 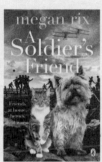

Chapter 1

Close to the white cliffs of Dover, a little German Shepherd puppy cowered away from the seagulls that circled menacingly above him. He'd tried to run away from the birds but they were bigger and faster than he was. He'd barked at them but the seagulls' cries only seemed to mock his high puppy yap.

Molly, a honey-coated spaniel, spotted the puppy and the gulls near the docks. She barked and ran at the large, sharp-beaked birds, scattering them into the drizzly sky of the early February morning. The gulls dodged the silver barrage balloons that floated high in the air, and circled to land on the warships anchored in the harbour, screeching in protest. But they didn't return.

Once they'd gone, the rain-soaked, floppy-eared, sable-coated puppy came over to his rescuer, whimpering and trembling with fear and cold. Molly licked his blue-eyed face to reassure him and he nuzzled into her. His pitiful cries were gradually calming but his desperate hunger remained.

Molly used her nose to knock over a glass bottle of milk that the milkman had just left at the Dover harbour master's door. The bottle smashed and the puppy's little pink tongue lapped thirstily at the milk that flowed on to the ground.

'Get away from that!' the milkman yelled angrily, when he saw the puppy drinking. His boot kicked out at him, only narrowly missing the puppy's little legs. Molly barked at the milkman and she and the pup ran off together with the milkman's furious shouts still ringing in their ears.

The smell of the sea and the reek of the oil from the ships grew fainter as they ran, but the small dog wasn't strong enough to run for very long yet, and they slowed to a walk as soon as they left the docks. Molly led the puppy through the outskirts of Dover to her den, a derelict garden shed at the edge of the allotments. There was sacking on the floor, it had a solid waterproof roof, and as an added bonus, every now and again a foolish rat or mouse would enter the shed – only to be pounced on and eagerly gulped down.

The tired puppy sank down on the sacking and immediately fell fast asleep, exhausted from the morning's excitement. Britain was in the grip of the Second World War, and Dover was a crucially important port, constantly filled with the hustle and bustle of ships and soldiers, but the puppy was blissfully unaware of all that.

Molly lay down too, her head resting on her paws, but she didn't sleep; she watched over her new companion.

Only a few weeks ago, Molly had been a much-loved pet, until a bomb had hit the house she lived in.

She remembered her owner being put on a stretcher and rushed to hospital, but Molly herself hadn't been found. She'd stayed hidden amid the rubble, shaking uncontrollably, too traumatized to make a sound.

She'd stayed in exactly the same spot for the rest of the night, covered in debris, too scared to sleep. At dawn she'd crawled out of her hiding place and taken her first tentative steps towards the shattered window and the world outside, alone.

The puppy snuffled in his sleep and Molly licked him gently until he settled. There were hundreds, maybe thousands, of lost and abandoned dogs in Dover but at least she and this baby Alsatian had found each other.

It all started with a Scarecrow

Puffin is over seventy years old.
Sounds ancient, doesn't it? But Puffin has never been
so lively. We're always on the lookout for the next big
idea, which is how it began all those years ago.

Penguin Books was a big idea from the mind of
a man called Allen Lane, who in 1935 invented
the quality paperback and changed the world.
**And from great Penguins, great Puffins grew,
changing the face of children's books forever.**

The first four Puffin Picture Books were hatched in 1940 and the
first Puffin story book featured a man with broomstick arms called
Worzel Gummidge. In 1967 Kaye Webb, Puffin Editor, started the
Puffin Club, promising to **'make children into readers'**.
She kept that promise and over 200,000 children became devoted
Puffineers through their quarterly instalments of *Puffin Post*.

Many years from now, we hope you'll look back and
remember Puffin with a smile. **No matter what your age
or what you're into, there's a Puffin for everyone.**
The possibilities are endless, but one thing is for sure:
whether it's a picture book or a paperback, a sticker book
or a hardback, **if it's got that little Puffin
on it – it's bound to be good.**